Imola the day after

Imola
The day after

Ilario Pax

Foreword

On May 1, 1994, at 6:40 p.m., Ayrton Senna succumbed to his injuries at the Maggiore Hospital in Bologna. A horrific crash at the Tamburello corner on the Imola circuit left him no chance. More than a quarter of a century after this tragedy, the memory of the Brazilian champion remains vivid in the minds of fans worldwide, including some who were not yet born at the time. His genius driving, extraordinary personality, and epic duel with Alain Prost undoubtedly contributed to this.

Today, the name Senna evokes performance, surpassing oneself, and legend. Even a supercar from the McLaren manufacturer, with whom he won his three world championship titles, bears his name. Cut down in the prime of his glory at only thirty-four years old, Ayrton Senna did not have time to complete a career that was already exceptional at the time of his death.

On that May 1, 1994, I was in front of my television. The tension at the start, after an already dramatic weekend, the image of his pulverized Williams-Renault, the long wait watching the rescuers bustling around him, all of that has remained etched forever in my mind. And then, in the early evening, the announcement of his death on the radio. It was like a cataclysm. We would never see the famous yellow helmet on a starting grid again. Unimaginable... And yet.

I must confess that at the time, I was not an unconditional fan of the Brazilian. Far from it. France was fortunate to have one of its own among the elite of Formula 1, and Senna was his fiercest rival. The battle between the two men was magnificent, intense, and sometimes violent. It was impossible to love one without hating the other and vice versa. On the evening of the 1993 Australian Grand Prix, Senna extended his hand to Prost for a welcome reconciliation. With the retirement of the Frenchman, the animosity between the two champions no longer made any sense. From that very powerful moment, I also started to perceive Ayrton Senna differently and to admire his talent in a more objective way. It is when they are no longer here that we sometimes realize how much certain people meant to us. That is exactly what I have felt since that fateful May 1, 1994. Since then, I have often wondered what the rest of his career and life would have been like if he had survived his accident. I will obviously never know the answer, but the magic of imagination knows no bounds.

In the following pages, I have incorporated a living Ayrton Senna into events that have actually taken place since his Imola accident. It is a parallel world in which the suspension triangle that killed him would have deviated from its trajectory by just a few centimeters, allowing him to survive.

Enjoy the read.

Ilario Pax

Imola, Sunday, May 1, 1994 , 2:17 p.m.

Packed in the stands lining the straight of the pit lane, the thousands of passionate tifosi catch a glimpse, for the fifth time that afternoon, of the Williams-Renault No. 2 emerging as the leader from the final chicane of the Imola circuit. Close on its heels, the Benetton-Ford driven by the young Michael Schumacher doesn't let it out of sight, ever since the safety car, which entered the track right after the start due to the collision between Lehto and Lamy, had pulled away. The first Ferrari, the one they all came to see on this first Sunday in May, is in third place but already at a considerable distance from the leading duo.

As the rest of the pack passes before their eyes, a sudden roar engulfs the crowd. The image that appears on the giant screen placed in front of them is staggering. Almost flat out in the terrifying left-hand curve of Tamburello, Ayrton Senna's single-seater suddenly deviates from the ideal trajectory and shoots straight ahead, crashing into the concrete wall that borders the circuit enclosure. At this spot, the run-off area is narrow despite the high speed of the F1 cars. The fault lies with a small stream that flows just behind the fences. Due to the ricochet effect, the Williams, or what remains of it, veers slightly to the right of the track before finally coming to a stop in the gravel. Under normal circumstances, the Italian crowd would have rejoiced at seeing the Brazilian driver retire, thus potentially offering a better result to the "Rossa" driven by Gerhard Berger. However, the previous day's fatal accident involving Roland Ratzenberger had paralyzed all the passionate fans of this sport who had not witnessed such a tragedy in racing for twelve years. Hypnotized by the wreckage of the Williams, the crowd holds its breath. The impact was extremely violent, and Senna has not yet emerged from his cockpit. After what feels like an eternity, lasting about twenty seconds, the champion finally removes his steering wheel and attempts to extricate himself from the mass of carbon fiber and metal surrounding him. However, dazed by the impact, he fails to climb over the shell of his car and sits back in his seat, waiting for the arrival of the medical team. A first rescuer approaches the famous yellow helmet:

- Are you okay? he shouts to him, trying to cover the noise of the other cars that come to a stop shortly after on the starting grid, as the red flag has been raised by the race direction.

- I think so, but I'm a bit dazed, the Brazilian responds in a breathless voice.

Freed from his helmet, he keeps his eyes closed for several long seconds, still sitting in the Williams. Then, having regained his composure, he straightens up and exits his cockpit from the right side, using the air intake above his head for support. His hand then encounters a piece of carbon debris. It's a component of his suspension triangle that had embedded itself like a knife into the bodywork of his car upon impact. If it had been just ten centimeters closer, it would have ended up in his visor.

- It didn't go far, he thinks to himself, regaining his full clarity as he notices the Austrian flag at his feet, which he had brought on board his machine at the start.

In the event of a victory, he had planned to wave it during his victory lap as a tribute to the driver who had tragically passed away during the qualifying session. The adrenaline of the competition had temporarily freed his mind from the image of the doctor's futile attempts to revive poor Roland Ratzenberger with a cardiac massage right there on the track. But sitting in the car that is taking him back to the medical center for routine examinations, he can't stop thinking about the unfortunate Simtek driver who lost his life right before his eyes twenty-four hours earlier.

He was exactly the same age as him but was only starting his F1 career in that year of 1994. In this small and also newly-established team, he wanted to make a name for himself. Just a few minutes before the end of the qualifying session, he chose to complete an additional fast lap instead of returning to the pit to have his car checked after going off-track. It turned out to be a grave mistake. Approaching the braking point of Tosa, he loses an aerodynamic component, likely damaged during the contact.

Suddenly destabilized, the Simtek spins out at 314 km/h and slams into the concrete wall, leaving no chance of survival for its driver.

With a third retirement in as many races, Senna strangely feels no frustration, despite being a fierce competitor at heart. Sporting considerations are miles away from his current concerns. This weekend, and his season start in general, has been a true nightmare. Even though he has finally acquired the ultimate weapon by taking the vacant seat left by Alain Prost at Williams-Renault, he fails to comprehend the behavior of his machine. He hasn't completed a single race since the beginning of the season, which is being dominated by the prodigy Schumacher, and the safety of the drivers is becoming increasingly uncertain. Since the start of the year, both JJ Lehto, a Benetton driver, and Jean Alesi have suffered serious accidents during private testing, temporarily keeping them away from the circuits.

Two days earlier, Rubens Barrichello, a 21-year-old Brazilian like Senna, had ended his practice session in the hospital with a broken nose and a sprained wrist after a spectacular crash. Ayrton was the first to visit him. He didn't hesitate to climb over a fence to bypass the prohibition of entering the medical center. Upon his return to the paddock, he took it upon himself to update the Brazilian press on Rubens' condition. Also born in São Paulo, Rubens had started his F1 career the previous year. Ayrton had taken him under his wing, and a bond of friendship was starting to form between the two men. In fact, the previous winter, they had spent a vacation together at Disneyland in Japan.

And then, on Saturday, the worst happened. A driver lost his life in the line of duty. Most of the rookies on the grid no longer imagined that they were defying death by lowering the visor of their helmets, as the last fatal accidents dated back several years. But Senna had not forgotten. Elio de Angelis, his teammate during his Lotus years, had been killed while driving his Brabham at the Paul Ricard circuit in 1986. It happened during a private testing session, which inevitably minimized the impact of the event at the time.

But the older ones still remember the charming smile of that young, talented Italian who chose racing out of passion, even though he could have lived a luxurious life by simply enjoying his family fortune.

After the accident, Ayrton felt somewhat guilty. Just a few hours earlier, while driving at a slow pace on the Provençal circuit, he had noticed the lack of rescue personnel compared to the usual setup during races. But caught up in his testing program, he had forgotten to relay the information. With more numerous and better-equipped rescuers, the life of the young Italian could have likely been saved. Clad in lightweight civilian attire, they were unable to approach the blazing wreckage of the Brabham in time to rescue the injured driver from that inferno.

Lost in his thoughts, Ayrton Senna snaps back to reality when Sid Watkins, the renowned doctor of Formula 1, taps on the car window upon their arrival at the medical center. Stepping into the small, rather outdated facility, he can't help but think that the safety of the drivers is not given enough consideration by the organizers of F1.

After a few examinations, the doctor, reassured, suggests taking him to the hospital in Bologna as a precautionary measure. But the champion, now feeling physically fine, refuses and heads towards his team's garage. Usually diligent in debriefing after a race, he can't wait to return to his Portuguese residence, where he stays during the European season of the championship. As he walks through the forest of microphones thrust towards him in the paddock, he doesn't respond to any of the questions the journalists try to ask him. His brother, Leonardo, who accompanies him to all the Grand Prix races, refuses to let him drive after such an impact and takes the wheel of the rental car provided for them.

The two men leave the confines of the Imola circuit while the race is not even finished. During the journey that takes them to the Forli airport, Ayrton Senna hardly says a word. He simply urges his brother to go faster. On the tarmac, he thanks Leonardo and bids him farewell. Leonardo cannot recall ever seeing Ayrton in such a state. Owen O'Mahoney, the pilot of his privately registered N125AS private jet, is waiting for him to take off towards the province of Algarve.

It is precisely 6:40 pm on his watch when he enters his luxurious villa in Quinta do Lago. Adriane Galisteu, his young companion, embraces him tightly upon seeing him enter. She had watched his horrifying crash live on television and had been very scared. Her joy at seeing him in one piece is intense, especially since their respective schedules had kept them apart for over a month. Ayrton explains that he is tired and wishes to be alone. Adriane doesn't insist. She knows he has been deeply affected by Ratzenberger's passing, and his own accident certainly hasn't improved his spirits.

Mechanically, he turns on the television to break the silence that fills his living room. It's time for Sunday night sports shows. On the screen, he discovers Michael Schumacher laughing on the podium with Nicola Larini and Mika Häkkinen by his side. The German has secured his third consecutive victory and has a 30-point lead over him in the championship. Feeling detached from what he sees, he pours himself a drink and collapses onto his couch. Completely drained, he eventually dozes off.

Night has completely fallen over Quinta do Lago when he abruptly wakes up, his forehead soaked in sweat and his heart pounding. In this awful nightmare that interrupted his sleep, he sees himself behind the wheel of the Williams heading straight into the Tamburello wall, unable to correct his trajectory. After regaining his composure, he remembers Nelson Piquet's statements a few years after his serious crash at the same spot in 1987. His sleep had been disturbed for a long time, while his compatriot claimed to be a heavy sleeper before that event.

He also sees himself with his friend Gerhard Berger at the very site of the crash. It was in 1990, a year after the Austrian's accident at the same spot. Berger's

Ferrari had lost its front wing and crashed straight into the wall. The fuel-filled tank had exploded upon impact and caught fire. Berger miraculously survived thanks to the swift intervention of rescuers. Becoming teammates at McLaren, they had returned to Tamburello in an attempt to improve the safety of that corner. However, the layout of the area prevented any modifications. They had parted ways somewhat resigned, saying to each other that someday someone would end up killing themselves against that damn concrete wall.

Quinta do Lago,

Friday, May 6, 1994, 11:30 AM

Ayrton Senna has not left his villa since returning from Imola. His body, still sore from the impact, continues to bother him a bit, but being young and athletic, he believes that after a few days of rest, everything will return to normal. However, from a mental standpoint, the Brazilian champion has never experienced such a period of doubt throughout his career. The repeated accidents, the difficulties in "understanding" his new car, and his lack of motivation are all new factors for him to manage.

Since Sunday, close friends and team members have been inquiring about his health over the phone. Despite his desire for isolation, he has responded to their concerns to avoid causing greater worry. However, the conversations have been brief, with Ayrton only reassuring them before cutting the calls short.

This morning, he woke up with a strong urge to talk to someone. But instead of dialing the number of a family member or his manager Julian Jakobi, he found himself dialing the number of his former arch-rival in the sport: Alain Prost.

The two men engaged in a fierce rivalry starting in

1988 when Ayrton became Prost's teammate at McLaren. Their rivalry reached its climax during the decisive 1990 Japanese Grand Prix for the championship title. Feeling cheated by being placed on the dirty side of the track for pole position, Ayrton had also not forgotten their collision that had cost him the title the previous year. For a year, he had been brooding, believing that Prost had intentionally taken him out of the race to secure the world championship for himself. Filled with resentment, he had started the race with the intention of colliding with the number 1 Ferrari if it entered the first corner of the Japanese circuit in the lead. We know the rest: the images of the McLaren and the Ferrari ending up in the gravel trap after just 500 meters circulated worldwide.

However, despite their fierce rivalry, Ayrton had taken the first step towards reconciliation on the podium of the 1993 Australian Grand Prix. On that day, he had won ahead of Alain, which turned out to be the final race of the "Professor's" career. As a sign of respect, Ayrton had invited him to join him on the top step. Since then, freed from the pressures of competition, they had started talking to each other again.

However, even though Ayrton thought he had achieved the ultimate goal by signing with the formidable Williams-Renault team, something was missing from the start of the year. In the absence of his lifelong rival, the sport he had loved so much and dedicated himself to no longer held the same appeal. He even expressed this longing the previous Saturday while commentating on a lap of the Imola circuit for the French broadcaster TF1. "*And to start, greetings to our friend Alain. We miss you, Alain!*" he declared into the microphone of TF1.

Convinced that only Prost could understand his numerous questions, he dialed the number of his predecessor at Williams.

- Hello Alain, it's Ayrton.

- Hi Ayrton, how are you feeling?

- I'm sore all over, but I'll recover.

- It's a minor injury considering the impact. Ratzenberger wasn't as fortunate as you.

- It's making me sick. Since Saturday, I can't get these horrific images out of my head.

- Perhaps we had forgotten too quickly that motorsport is dangerous.

- Will you attend his funeral tomorrow?

- Yes, many will be present. Niki called me. He wanted me to join the other drivers.

- Personally, I don't feel up to it. Please convey the message that I will be with you all in spirit and that I'm praying for Roland and his loved ones.

- Don't worry about that and rest, you really need it.

- You know, Alain, all these events have shaken me up. I'm 30 points behind Schumacher after three Grand Prix races, and it doesn't bother me at all. When I used to race against you, just seeing you ahead of me, even by a few points, made me mad. I don't recognize myself anymore.

- You are still caught up in the emotion, and that's normal. In a few days, your competitive spirit will resurface.

- I'll tell you something. Even before this cursed weekend, I was already feeling a certain weariness, and I believe your absence had a lot to do with it. The two of us were interconnected. For years, fighting against you was my only goal. One's career means nothing without the other's.

- It's true, we didn't give each other any gifts.

- On that note, I was too proud to tell you, but today I want to apologize for Suzuka. Looking back, I realize that my gesture was senseless. At that speed, I could have killed you.

- I held a deep grudge against you for that, and you know it. But that's all in the past, and as you can see, I'm very much alive! And between us, you deserved that championship, just as I deserved the one in 1989. In the end, everything fell into place.

- You might be right, but with what happened on Saturday, I realize that I was completely reckless that day. No world title is worth putting one's life and the lives of others at risk.

- Don't dwell on it anymore. I suggest we continue this conversation in Monaco. I need to prepare myself. My flight to Salzburg takes off in three hours.

- Okay, Alain. See you very soon.

- Until then, Ayrton.

Monaco, Wednesday, May 11, 1994, 4:00 PM

Sitting on the wall that borders the stands of the Monaco circuit, Ayrton Senna appears lost in thought. Eleven days have passed since his crash at Imola. Fully recovered physically, he has been given clearance by the FIA doctor to get back behind the wheel of his Williams. The first free practice sessions for the Monaco Grand Prix will begin the next morning. He knows this track like the back of his hand and has won six of the last seven editions. It's safe to say he is the king of the Principality.

His press attaché approaches him to remind him that the pre-race press conference is about to begin. Silent since Imola, he knows he will have to face the pack of journalists eager for his comments on his accident. Somewhat reluctantly, he heads towards the media center. On his way, he encounters a familiar face. It's Lionel Froissart, a journalist from the French newspaper *Libération* who has been following him since his karting days and with whom he has forged a special bond.

- Hello Lionel, Ayrton greets him in nearly accent-free French.

- Ah, Ayrton! I'm glad to see you in good shape. You gave us quite a scare at Imola!

- My lucky star was watching over me, but for how long? the Williams driver sighs, visibly upset.

- We're going through a tough period indeed.

- Perhaps we've had too much luck in recent years and we've become a bit complacent. The warnings were there, though. Gerhard in '89, Donnelly in Jerez in '90. And those fuel stops. One day it will end badly.

- You're now the most experienced driver on the grid. Your voice matters. It's up to you to use your status to try and improve safety.

- I'm a bit tired of fighting against the sporting authorities. Remember what happened with Balestre.

- Exactly, he's no longer here. And who better than a driver, especially the only active world champion, to propose avenues for improvement? In his time, Jackie Stewart did a lot of work, and his fight certainly saved lives.

- I agree with you, Lionel, but for now, I don't really have the head for it. We need to let the emotional time pass, concludes the Brazilian as he enters the press room.

However, as he had suggested to Erik Comas at

Imola, Ayrton decides to organize an informal meeting among the drivers following the press conference. Several of his colleagues, who hadn't seen him since his crash, start by asking about his physical condition.

- Apart from a slight stiffness in my neck, I've fully recovered, the Brazilian replies. But Roland wasn't as lucky, and others among us came very close to catastrophe.

- The cars have become indestructible, and it's the body that absorbs all the energy of the impact, Jean Alesi adds, making his return to Monaco after being involved in an accident himself. The doctors who treated me said I could have suffered severe consequences, even paralysis. I also had a lot of luck.

- The neck has become our weak point. I've heard about a head restraint system being studied in the United States that could prevent whiplash, Mark Blundell announces. The problem is that it's not yet approved.

- I can't imagine driving without being completely free in my movements, Martin Brundle responds, clearly unconvinced by this invention.

Senna then takes control of the discussion:

- For me, the most urgent thing is to inspect the runoff areas and find out what exists in terms of impact absorbers. At Imola, Roland

and I hit the concrete directly at very high speed. We need to avoid that as much as possible in the future.

- No matter what we do, Formula 1 will always be a dangerous sport. We all know that. If we're no longer willing to take these risks, it's better to quit, Michael Schumacher declares.

The timing is probably poorly chosen by the young German driver, but he seizes this opportunity to solidify the psychological war between him and Senna. For the first time in his career, he has a chance to compete for the world title, and he intends to use every means to destabilize his opponent, even though safety concerns naturally occupy his mind.

- We all agree that motorsport will always be dangerous, that's not the question, Gerhard Berger retorts, sensing the growing annoyance on Ayrton's face. But if we remain idle, we are heading towards disasters. The circuits are becoming less and less suited to the speed of our cars, and it must be possible to make improvements.

Considerably irritated by Schumacher's attitude, Senna finally cuts short the discussion and prefers to join his team to get to work. He is finding it increasingly difficult to understand the arrogance of the Benetton driver, with whom he has had a few verbal and even physical clashes in the past.

The dispute between the two men dates back to the 1992 season. It began with a misunderstanding at the

Brazilian Grand Prix. Senna was running third ahead of Schumacher early in the race when he started experiencing engine cutouts. He signaled to the Benetton driver that he had a problem. Schumacher, thinking that Senna was intentionally slowing down at certain parts of the circuit, didn't hesitate to accuse the Brazilian of unsportsmanlike behavior during the post-race press conference. However, Senna's issues were genuine, and he was forced to retire. This public statement discrediting him, especially in his home country of Brazil, greatly irritated him.

At Magny-Cours, a few weeks later, Schumacher collided with Senna's McLaren at the first corner of Adelaide, further fueling the tension between the two men.

The climax of their conflict occurred during the qualifying session of the German Grand Prix. Wanting to provoke his rival, the German driver abruptly hit the brakes right in front of Senna's red and white car at the entrance to the pit lane. Outraged by this foolish and dangerous maneuver, Senna then rushed towards the Benetton pit to express his thoughts to Schumacher. Without the intervention of the team mechanics, the two drivers would likely have come to blows.

Since those incidents, they had met privately to clarify matters, and their relationship had calmed down. But while respecting the talent of the younger driver, Ayrton struggled to understand the behavior of this new generation. He perhaps forgot that he himself had not always displayed exemplary conduct during his career.

Monaco, Thursday, May 12, 1994, First Free Practice Session

Dressed in his racing overalls, with his famous Nacional bank cap firmly on his head, Ayrton appears in the Williams pit. The first practice session of the Grand Prix is about to begin in a few moments. He hasn't sat in the cockpit of his single-seater since his accident, but the instincts quickly return. First, the helmet, that famous yellow helmet representing his homeland and contributing to his legend. Then he sits in the cockpit, and his mechanics help him tighten his harness. All that's left is to put on his gloves, and he'll be ready to hit the track. His car is identical in every way to the one that was destroyed in Imola. Only the sticker "For Roland" placed on the airbox revives the sad memory of the Austrian's passing.

In his rearview mirrors, the engine attendant signals him to start. Suddenly, the cramped space dedicated to car preparation begins to tremble due to the deafening noise produced by the Renault V10 engine. First gear engaged, Ayrton fixes his gaze on the mechanic, who scans the pit lane to send him out safely. Gerhard Berger's Ferrari passes in front of him, and then he signals to the young man that the coast is clear. The Williams smoothly exits the garage, climbs the pit lane, and then accelerates rapidly towards the Sainte-Dévote corner.

The session lasts an hour and a half. Immersed in the adjustments he needs to make to prepare for the Grand Prix, he is in his element and has no time to dwell. He has regained the sensations he loves above all: pushing the limits between the rails of the Monaco carousel.

"At least here, with the low average speed, we should avoid another catastrophe," he thinks to himself as he gets out of his car, with about half an hour left in the session. That's when his attention is drawn to the television screen in front of him. He sees the marshals waving yellow flags at the harbor chicane. Karl Wendlinger's Sauber has gone off track and ended up in the escape road. The fastest section of the circuit is located after the tunnel. The loss of control by Wendlinger is replayed by the broadcast director. In real time, the image is chilling. The Sauber is destabilized by a curb and slides for a long time perpendicular to the track. Out of control, the car crashes into the tire wall in front of the barrier separating the escape road from the Monaco track. The head of the great Austrian driver juts out in an exaggerated manner above the Sauber's cockpit. Without protection, it strikes the tires at full speed.

Ayrton can't take his eyes off the screen. The Monaco track marshals are considered the best in the championship. In just a few seconds, they are at the bedside of the unconscious driver. Like a horrific never-ending nightmare, Ayrton sees the same images he witnessed fifteen days ago in Imola. The images of a medical team busy around an unconscious driver. After long agonizing minutes, Wendlinger is taken to the Saint-Roch Hospital in Nice, where a team of neurologists will take care of him.

On-site, the examinations conducted on the injured driver deliver their terrible verdict. He has no fractures, but a cerebral edema is compressing his brain. The doctors can do nothing but sedate him and wait. His life is in danger. When Ayrton learns the news, he isolates himself in his team's motorhome. His body refuses to accept any more tragedies, and he is overcome by violent spasms and vomiting. Unlike what he did in Imola after Ratzenberger's accident or in Jerez in 1990 for Martin Donnelly, he is unable to go to the scene to understand.

At this moment, he would like to be somewhere else, far from this circuit, far from these racing cars that have built his legend and now resemble a massacre game. Journalists await him outside the motorhome to gather his comments. An unusual commotion can be felt, with several team members coming in and out without saying a word. Suddenly, the door opens, and Ayrton, wearing jeans and a Williams team-colored shirt, appears before them. Microphones are thrust towards the Brazilian as all eyes turn to him. His statement is brief. He invites them to join him for an impromptu press conference at 1 p.m. in the press room and then disappears into the garage. For long minutes, television cameras try to capture some images. A fleeting glimpse of Ayrton engaged in a serious discussion with Frank Williams and his partner, Patrick Head, is caught on screen. Amidst the crowd of journalists, rumors of the Grand Prix being canceled circulate. 1 p.m. approaches, and soon they will have their answers.

The press room at the Monaco circuit had never experienced such excitement. A few minutes behind schedule, Ayrton Senna steps onto the stage. His entrance is greeted by a flurry of camera flashes. With a serious demeanor, he takes his seat at the table. Patrick Head is to his left, Frank Williams to his right. He pours a glass of water and takes a sip. The silence in the room is overwhelming. Gazing into the distance, Senna brings the microphone to his lips and begins his statement.

"I have called you all here this afternoon due to the dramatic circumstances that you are all aware of. Formula One has lost one of its own less than fifteen days ago at Imola, and another is fighting to stay alive as I speak. I myself miraculously emerged unscathed from my crash at Imola. All these events have deeply shaken me and severely eroded my confidence... Under these circumstances, I have made the decision, in agreement with Frank and Patrick here present, not to participate in the race on Sunday..."

A clamor suddenly fills the room. For Formula One observers, it is a shock. No one had imagined such a scenario. Once the calm returns, Senna continues, his eyes reddened with emotion:

"... Furthermore, I announce to you that my Formula One career ends today as I have decided to retire from the sport with immediate effect. I bitterly regret that this happens at such a dramatic moment, but auto racing is an incredibly demanding sport, and I feel that I am no longer in the appropriate psychological condition to continue practicing my profession."

This time, the journalists are left speechless. This announcement has the effect of a tsunami.

"Formula One has brought me immense satisfaction and has been my sole reason for living for 10 years, but today, weariness and sadness have overshadowed my competitive drive. I have loved and will always love this sport, but I need to take a step back, and I hope my fans will understand. Thank you for your attention, and I now pass the floor to Frank."

Ayrton Senna passes the microphone to his employer, but Frank Williams is immediately interrupted by the cascade of questions directed at his driver, coming from the assembly. His press attaché is forced to play the role of a police officer to discipline the dozens of journalists present.

-   Ayrton, wasn't this decision made hastily under special circumstances, and is it truly irrevocable? asks a Brazilian journalist from TV Globo, almost as emotional as the driver himself.

-   My desire to retire has been growing gradually since the beginning of the season. Certainly, the tragedies and my accident have accelerated things, but I believe that today it is the best decision considering my current state of mind. As for whether it is irrevocable; at this moment, I would say yes.

-   You have the best car, and you are only 34 years old. Aren't you afraid of regretting this choice in the weeks to come? ventures a

British journalist.

- It's not a question of age but rather of commitment and mindset. In my car, I risk my life, and there is no question of driving without being 100% focused on those aspects. Of course, the adrenaline of competition and pushing the limits will certainly be missed. It's up to me to find ways to compensate for this loss. But at this moment, there are more serious things that concern me.

After this final response, the Brazilian champion sets down his microphone and exits the press room through a hidden door. An official from the Automobile Club de Monaco believes he sees a tear rolling down his cheek at that moment.

Le Mans, Sunday, June 19, 1994

A month had passed since the announcement of his retirement from racing. Far from the turmoil of Formula 1, Ayrton had found some serenity in his vast Brazilian estate. He was also relieved to learn that Karl Wendlinger's health was improving. At Williams, David Coulthard, who had been a test driver, was promoted to the number 2 seat. Imagine the young Scot's surprise when he picked up the phone a few hours before his departure for Catalonia. He immediately recognized the voice of the Brazilian, who simply wanted to wish him good luck for his debut in the sport.

In Barcelona, two weeks after Michael Schumacher's fourth consecutive victory at the Monaco Grand Prix, Damon Hill finally broke the German prodigy's dominance and claimed his first win of the season. While he was happy for his former teammate, this event did not fuel any regrets about his abrupt decision to retire. However, the news that Karl Wendlinger had come out of a coma brought a mixed feeling of joy and relief. Although the Austrian was about to embark on a long and difficult rehabilitation period, at least he had survived.

Freed from any commitments, Ayrton took the opportunity to accelerate the development of his foundation aimed at helping underprivileged children in the Brazilian favelas. With the assistance of Ron Dennis, he was able to register the foundation's statutes in the UK in less than two weeks. Doing it in Brazil would have taken him months due to the administrative burden plaguing the country. His sister, Viviane, joined him in this ambitious project. In search of funding, he had published a comic book earlier in the year titled "Senninha," featuring a hero who closely resembled a famous Brazilian driver with a yellow helmet. It was as an ambassador for this foundation that he made the trip to Le Mans to promote it to the public. He could have done it during a Grand Prix weekend, but he felt it was still too early to return to the F1 atmosphere. Besides, aren't the 24 Hours of Le Mans the greatest endurance race in the world with enormous media exposure?

However, during his racing career, he had never attended this event, and the world of endurance racing was completely unknown to him. Only once, in 1984, did he participate in the 1000km of Nürburgring in a Porsche 956 alongside Henri Pescarolo and Stefan Johansson, but the relentless attacker that he was did not have a great memory of that experience.

As one could imagine, the presence of the Brazilian triple world champion in the paddock of the Sarthe circuit attracted a swarm of journalists, and that's exactly what he came for, but for a good cause. Willingly, he engages in a question-and-answer session with the press. Naturally, most of the questions revolve around his recent retirement and a possible future in other sports categories, and Ayrton struggles to steer the conversation towards his foundation. Nonetheless, he manages to get his message across and takes advantage of his presence in Sarthe to get to know this legendary race. As the motorsport enthusiast that he is, he wanders from garage to garage, quenching his interlocutors' thirst for questions. In doing so, he encounters several familiar faces that he had crossed paths with during his career. Eric Van de Poele, René Arnoux, and Bertrand Gachot are participating in the event and had interacted with Ayrton in the F1 paddocks. However, when he was active, he never took the time to engage in dialogue with them, let alone make friends. It was his way of staying focused and not mixing competition with friendship. However, when he enters the garage of car number 35, a radiant smile suddenly lights up his face. The Belgian Thierry Boutsen, who retired from F1 at the end of the 1993 season, is replenishing himself after a long stint behind the wheel of the Dauer-Porsche. Their friendship dates back about ten years, to the time when they were starting in Grand Prix racing. Along with Gerhard Berger, he is one of the few drivers who was truly close to Ayrton Senna. In fact, Ayrton has agreed to become the godfather of Thierry's newborn son, Cédric, born just a few days ago. Delighted to be together, the two men embrace and chat for a good twenty minutes, with photographers capturing the moment, before the Brazilian champion takes his leave so as not to disturb his friend's race too much.

As the hours pass, Ayrton gets caught up in the game and diligently follows the progress of the race. When the number 1 Toyota, which seemed to have the race won, enters the pits less than half an hour before the finish, he remains captivated in front of a television screen and discovers the drama of the 24 Hours that made its legend.

At the finish, he is invited by officials, seeking captivating images, to step onto the podium and present the trophy to the winners. From the elevated structure compared to the track, he is enthralled by the enormous crowd of enthusiasts who gather to celebrate their heroes. He had never experienced such enthusiasm in Formula 1, except perhaps at Interlagos when he finally won his home Grand Prix in 1991. Just by recalling that fantastic memory, he feels shivers running through his body. He remembers that it is also for experiencing emotions like these that he chose to lead the life of a racing driver.

On the third step of the podium, he joyfully reunites with his friend Boutsen, accompanied by his two teammates, Hans-Joachim Stuck and Danny Sullivan. However, he is much less enthusiastic about seeing Eddie Irvine, who finished second in the race alongside Mauro Martini and Jeff Krosnoff. The Irishman, who had made a thunderous debut in F1 the previous year in Suzuka, had left him with bad memory. While attempting to lap him in pouring rain, the Jordan driver had needlessly put up a fight. Tempers flared at the finish, and Ayrton, losing his cool, punched him in the face. This regrettable gesture had earned him a suspended sentence from the FIA. Irvine, being the fiery young driver that he is, had once again made headlines at the beginning of the season in Interlagos. Judged responsible for a pile-up involving Jos Verstappen, Eric Bernard, and Martin Brundle, he received a one-race suspension, which was increased to three races due to his provocative behavior during the appeal hearing. Needless to say, the obligatory handshake between the two men is more than icy. Fortunately, the winning crew composed of Frenchman Yannick Dalmas, American Hurley Haywood, and Italian Mauro Baldi arrives to the cheers of the crowd. After the national anthems ceremony, Ayrton hands the trophy to the driver from Var, who celebrates his second victory in the Le Mans classic, while his American teammate can now boast of being on the Le Mans podium three times.

It is only late in the evening that Ayrton finally leaves the Bugatti Circuit after lingering in endless technical discussions with his friend Thierry Boutsen and then with Yannick Dalmas, who joined them once his obligations as a winner were fulfilled. Despite his abrupt decision to retire from F1, the passion for racing had not left him.

Woking, Wednesday, November 16, 1994

While on a business trip to Great Britain, Ayrton Senna visits the McLaren factory in Woking at the invitation of Ron Dennis. The famous team boss, with whom he has achieved so much success, awaits him in his office. On the way, Ayrton imagines that old Ron will once again try to convince him to come out of retirement and drive one of his cars in the following season. Hadn't he already tried to change his mind at the end of the 1993 Australian Grand Prix when he had already signed a contract with Williams? Although he has no intention of diving back into the deep end, he is genuinely pleased to see his friend again as he passes through the entrance gate of the ultra-modern factory.

Within these premises, he feels somewhat at home. You don't spend six seasons in a team, punctuated by three world championship titles, without leaving an indelible mark. The human warmth that permeates these places is not a legend, and as he is greeted by the staff from all directions, it takes him a good fifteen minutes to finally reach the door of the boss's office.

- Hey Ron! he exclaims as he enters the brightly lit room.

- Ah, Ayrton! There you are! It's so good to see you again after these long months of silence.

- You know, I needed to cut ties with F1 and the creation of my foundation takes up a lot of my time. Fortunately, Viviane is there to help me.

- I won't beat around the bush, Ayrton. If I asked you to come, it's not just to reminisce about the good old days.

- You're incorrigible, Ron! But I'm definitely going to disappoint you. There's absolutely no way I'm going back to the paddocks.

- I'm the first one disappointed, but I expected that answer. To be honest with you, Alain already informed me that you weren't considering a comeback.

- And I suppose you offered him the same thing.

- It would be a professional mistake not to! You both brought so much to the team! Dennis responds with a burst of laughter before regaining his seriousness. Actually, I wanted you to come to visit the factory.

- Visit the factory? Ayrton exclaims. But I've spent so many days and nights there in six years that I know every nook and cranny.

- Come with me anyway, Dennis concludes,

taking his former driver by the arm.

To the great surprise of the Brazilian, his former boss doesn't lead him to the Formula 1 car assembly workshops, but rather to the assembly lines of the McLaren F1 road cars that the team has been marketing for a few months.

There, in a corner of the building, a car is covered with a McLaren-colored tarp. Ron Dennis approaches it and, while unveiling the car to his former champion, proudly addresses him:

-   Allow me to introduce the McLaren F1 GTR, the race version of our supercar that you know well. We will enter it in the BPR Championship next year. The highlight of the season will be the 24 Hours of Le Mans, where we will entrust seven cars to private teams to race them. The Kokusai Kaihatsu Racing team has already enlisted Masanori Sekiya and the reigning champion of the event, the Frenchman Yannick Dalmas, whom you met last June during your visit to Le Mans. I heard that you showed particular interested during your conversations after the race

-   Where are you going with this, Ron?

-   You're not unaware that the 24 Hours of Le Mans are raced with three-driver lineups. I simply offer you the last vacant seat in that car.

- I don't know what to say. It's so unexpected.

- If it helps you make a decision, know that the regulations will favor the GT cars, which will make up 80% of the field. Overall victory is entirely possible.
- Sure, I was completely fascinated by the atmosphere of the event, but my only participation in an endurance race in '84 at the Nürburgring wasn't a particularly thrilling experience.

- Yes, I know you told Pescarolo, after beating him by over two seconds per lap, that it was too heavy and too slow for you.

- I didn't remember that, but indeed I could have said that.

- That was 10 years ago, and you were just starting your F1 career. But today, you've retired and gained experience. What I'm offering you is a real chance for victory in the greatest endurance race in the world, and especially in a car from the brand with which you won almost everything. Admit that the story would be beautiful!

- You have a way of magnifying things, Ron! Looking at it that way, I can only say that it deserves consideration.

- I would add that the average speed will be

much lower than with the prototypes, which will minimize the risks of serious accidents.

- Do you still have more arguments up your sleeve? Ayrton cuts in, casting a mischievous glance at his interlocutor.

- You're right, I'll save some for lunch, which awaits us. Follow me, I'm starving.

Silverstone Circuit, Tuesday, March 21, 1995

"McLaren Technology and Lanzante Motorsport are pleased to invite you to the Silverstone Circuit on Tuesday, March 21, 1995, at 11 o'clock for the presentation of the crew of McLaren F1 GTR No. 59, who will compete in the 63rd edition of the 24 Hours of Le Mans on June 17th and 18th."

With this concise announcement, the specialized press is invited to attend on a misty spring morning. At first glance, it may not seem like a rush for a journalist experienced in such events.

However, a crowd gathers at the gates of the venerable British circuit, creating an atmosphere of excitement. Amidst the buzz, one name dominates every conversation: "Senna." The information has been kept secret, but leaks and the choice of date, which coincides with the Brazilian's 35th birthday, have convinced even the skeptics not to miss this appointment.

The show takes place on the start/finish line of the circuit. On a small platform, the outline of a McLaren F1 can be vaguely seen, partially concealed by a large black sheet. However, the journalists have not come for the car. In the foreground, Paul Lanzante and Ron Dennis wait for the entire audience to be seated before beginning their speeches.

Finally, as silence falls, Paul Lanzante takes the floor to present the technical specifications of the F1 GTR. Complying with the GT regulations, the car is largely based on the production model. It is powered by a 6.1-liter, 60-degree V12 BMW engine, producing 607 hp, which is 20 hp less than the road version to comply with the regulations. It also features a reinforced gearbox and carbon brakes. Ron Dennis then takes over to announce that six additional McLaren F1 GTRs will be entered, with the ultimate ambition of claiming victory.

Then comes the highly anticipated moment of the driver presentation. The first to be called is 45-year-old Masanori Sekiya from Japan. He has already participated in the 24 Hours of Le Mans eight times, mainly driving for Toyota, with a second-place finish in 1992 as his best result.

Yannick Dalmas, 33 years old, makes his appearance next. The driver from Var has competed in 24 Formula 1 Grand Prix races between 1987 and 1994. However, he has already won the Le Mans classic twice, in 1992 with Peugeot and the previous year with a Dauer 962-Porsche.

The moment everyone has been waiting for is approaching. Ron Dennis takes the microphone again and is about to announce the name of the last driver of the team.

- With him, I have experienced my greatest professional and sporting satisfactions. I am extremely proud to have convinced him to embark on this magnificent adventure, and I am certain that his talent and dedication will ardently contribute to its success. I won't keep you in suspense any longer since you have already guessed it: Ayrton Senna will participate in his first 24 Hours of Le Mans in this car.

Dressed in a white suit with the colors of the team's Japanese sponsor, Ayrton Senna then takes his place alongside the other two drivers amid the enthusiastic applause of the journalists. A cap with the red 'Senna' emblem has replaced his famous Banco Nacional sponsor, which is facing serious financial difficulties.

Amidst the flashing cameras, the three drivers unveil their car, which sports a black livery and the name of a Japanese plastic surgery clinic. The logo of the comic book hero 'Senninha' prominently appears on the rear wings. Ayrton attached great importance to this exposure to strengthen the funding for his foundation.

Sekiya and Dalmas answer the initial questions from reporters, but as expected, the Paulista is the most sought after of the three.

- First of all, Ayrton, let me wish you a happy birthday. What prompted you to return to the race track after almost a year of inactivity? begins a British journalist.

- To be honest, I hadn't considered getting back behind the wheel of a race car for now.

The development of my foundation for Brazilian children takes up a large part of my time, but that crafty old Ron managed to find the right words to make me eventually agree to follow him.

- Was participating in the 24 Hours of Le Mans part of your career plans? a female voice follows up.

- Along with the Monaco Grand Prix and the Indianapolis 500, Le Mans is one of the three pillars of motorsport, but my attacking temperament is more in line with the other two events. It was during my visit to the 1994 edition that I caught the bug. The atmosphere is extraordinary and unique, and I must give a big thank you to Yannick, with whom I had a long conversation after his victory. His passionate explanations of what makes the essence of the 24 Hours greatly contributed to my interest in this race.

- What are your ambitions for this first participation?

- I still don't know what my level will be in this discipline where I have everything to learn, but behind the wheel of a McLaren and with a double winner as my teammate, we can only aim for a great result. Victory would obviously be magical, but I dare not believe in it just yet.

The Q&A session will last for another half-hour, and without Ron Dennis's intervention, it could have gone on even longer. This participation is generating the keenest interest from observers, delighting the renowned team boss from Woking.

Thruxton Circuit, Saturday, April 15, 1995

On this spring morning, an unusual excitement fills the air in front of the gates of Thruxton Circuit in southern England. About twenty Ayrton Senna fans have been waiting since sunrise in the hope of catching a glimpse of their idol. McLaren has reserved the circuit for a race simulation with car number 59 in preparation for the upcoming 24 Hours of Le Mans. With nearly 40% of the team's staff being McLaren employees, it's somewhat like a "factory" car, even though it is entered by a private structure. Initially, this session was supposed to take place at the Magny-Cours circuit in Burgundy, France, but only for 21 hours due to noise restrictions imposed by the neighboring community. Upon learning this, Ayrton promptly called Ron Dennis to convince him to change the track so they could truly run for 24 hours. Thanks to his persuasive abilities and, of course, his aura, he ultimately succeeded, and thus, the test is set to begin on this English circuit this morning.

Suddenly, behind the wheel of a rented, imposing BMW 5 Series, a familiar figure catches the attention of the group. It's Ayrton Senna. He is the first to arrive at this circuit, which he hadn't seen since the early '80s. At that time, he was racing in British F3 with hopes of building a successful Formula 1 career.

Returning to this place brings back memories of his arrival in this distant country at just 20 years old, determined to give himself the best chances of shining in motorsport. Back then, the Brazilian exile community in the UK stuck together to establish themselves on the old continent. Chico Serra, a slightly older driver, had welcomed him upon his arrival in London in late 1980 and introduced him to the world of Formula Ford, where Ayrton would begin his automotive career in a remarkable fashion. A few years later, like a passing of the torch, he would take young Mauricio Gugelmin under his wing. Thruxton Circuit undoubtedly reminds him of his fantastic 1983 F3 season, in which he won the championship after a fierce battle against Martin Brundle. The following year, both men made the leap to Formula 1 together, but the British driver wouldn't gather as many trophies as his illustrious rival.

Overwhelmed by fans seeking autographs and photos of their idol, Ayrton doesn't have the heart to deny them this happiness. He parks his car and gives them a memorable fifteen minutes. But he doesn't forget the reason for his presence here this morning. An arduous yet necessary weekend of work awaits him, and being the perfectionist he is, he politely bids farewell to his audience to quickly rejoin his racing team.

Seven McLaren engineers have been sent as reinforcements to assist the Lanzante Motorsport team responsible for fielding the McLaren F1 GTR No. 59. His appearance in the pit area makes an impression. It's not every day that the technicians from this small outfit come across a three-time Formula 1 world champion.

Eighteen months after his departure from the Woking team, he joyfully reunites with some familiar faces and promptly goes to warmly greet them. Just as he had always done when joining a new team, he proceeds to have each person he will be working with introduced to him one by one. In Formula 1, it was a way for him to understand each individual's specific role and, incidentally, to win the sympathy of his men in an attempt to gain an advantage over his teammates. The difference here is that they all work on the same car that Ayrton will have to share with two other drivers. This approach is entirely unprecedented for him, and that is precisely why this testing session feels absolutely necessary.

Although the start of this simulation is scheduled for 4 p.m., and his first stint doesn't begin until two hours later, Ayrton immediately goes to change and put on his racing suit. It's his way of diving right into the heart of the matter. For an hour, he goes over the functioning of the car in detail, even though a similar briefing had taken place a few weeks prior at the factory. His meticulous nature demands this thorough review; a way for him to have complete control and avoid any uncomfortable situations during the race.

Nearly two hours after his arrival, Masanori Sekiya and Yannick Dalmas make their appearance at the originally scheduled time. They are surprised to see Senna already in his gear, engaged in a discussion with the track engineer. Dalmas, who had conducted tests for McLaren-Peugeot the previous year, is familiar with Senna's working methods, as shared by some technicians. He whispers to Sekiya:

- He's true to himself and wants to know everything before hitting the track. It's a good sign for us; he takes this challenge very seriously.

Absorbed in their conversation, Ayrton hasn't noticed their arrival. Despite being in the same profession, the two men hesitate to interrupt and greet him. Senna has always maintained a certain distance between himself and other drivers, and his personality commands respect. He's not the type of man you casually tap on the shoulder. After a few seconds, their gazes finally meet, and he warmly greets his co-drivers with a firm handshake.

The day's schedule is meticulously planned. After a technical briefing, outlining the elements to be tested during the simulation, the crew will have a snack before the departure of the first driver, Yannick Dalmas, the most experienced among them.

Although it's a minor detail, this choice slightly bothers the Brazilian, who is eager to experience his machine. His reflexes as a self-centered and even temperamental single-seater driver resurface. What was a quality in Formula 1 can become a handicap in a team race. The team manager kindly but firmly reminds him that endurance racing is a team sport, and in any case, the driving times will be the same for all three drivers over the course of these 24 hours. With this small discomfort cleared, the entire team leaves the pit for a meal. They know it's their last true moment of relaxation for the weekend and intend to enjoy this meal.

At exactly 4 p.m., Yannick Dalmas begins his first two-hour stint. Meanwhile, Ayrton engages in conversation with the track engineer, who inundates him with advice while scrutinizing telemetry data. Race pace, fuel consumption, pit stops, overtaking slower cars, rest times, Paulista wants to know everything. He is so absorbed in the discussion that he almost forgets his own upcoming stint.

Gloved and helmeted, Ayrton watches the black McLaren approach the pit lane. Yannick Dalmas positions the car precisely between the markings on the ground, indicating his spot. Immediately, Ayrton opens the door and helps his teammate unfasten his harness. In less than five seconds, the driver is out, and his renowned teammate jumps into the seat. This time, it's Dalmas who assists in tightening Ayrton's safety harness. With the refueling completed, they're off for two hours of non-stop driving.

After completing a moderate-paced installation lap, Ayrton picks up the pace while sharing his initial impressions. On his fifth lap, he beats Dalmas' best lap time. The following lap, he improves it by another five tenths. Through the radio, the track engineer reminds him to adhere to the predetermined race pace. As a natural-born attacker, he is asked to drive against his instincts. Endurance racing is a delicate balance of speed, tire conservation, fuel management, and mechanical preservation. Although reluctant, he understands the importance of complying and slows down.

At 8:00 p.m., the signaller orders him to return to the pit for the second driver change. It is now Masanori Sekiya's turn to take the wheel of the McLaren. After some stretching to relax, he eagerly goes to debrief the first stint with Yannick Dalmas. The engineer analyzes the fuel consumption figures of both drivers. At an equivalent pace, the Brazilian shows a 15% higher fuel consumption compared to the Frenchman. Moreover, he has been harder on his brakes, and a brake pad replacement will be needed sooner than expected. Senna is astonished when he reads these numbers:

- I don't understand. I thought I was driving economically.

- You see, Ayrton, you need to completely reconsider your driving style. In Formula 1, aggression often pays off, but here, don't hesitate to lose a bit of time in order to gain in the end. For example, you can ease off the throttle a few tenths or even one or two seconds before braking. These small actions, repeated hundreds of times, save fuel. There's no point in taking risks to gain one second per lap and lose that advantage by needing an extra pit stop, explains Yannick Dalmas.

- I realize that endurance racing is full of subtleties, and I still have a lot to learn.

- Don't worry, Ayrton, all these automatic
adjustments will come. It was the same for me
when I started at Le Mans, I had the wrong
reflexes from Formula 1.

With his next stint scheduled for midnight, Senna
decides to grab a bite to eat before resting for a few
hours in the team's motorhome. When he returns to
the track, it's pitch black, yet another new factor to
incorporate into his learning process. In the
meantime, the McLaren undergoes a minor pit stop to
replace the brake pads and resolve a sticky throttle
issue. However, unexpectedly, Ayrton returns to the
pit after only two laps.

- The car doesn't behave the same way during
braking, he explains to the technician who
came to inquire about the cause of his stop. I
feel like the issue is coming from the front
right.

After checking, the man returns to the side of the
driver, still strapped into the car.

- Indeed, you're right. We fitted slightly worn
brake pads on the front right after a few tens
of kilometers of running last week, while the
others are completely new. You can continue;
there are no problems. After a few laps,
everything will be back to normal.

Assured, Senna lowers his visor, shifts into first gear,
and disappears into the cool night of Hampshire.
Informed of the anecdote, the track engineer is

impressed by his driver's technical sensitivity. His reputation was well deserved, and then some.

The rest of the night goes by without notable issues. In the early morning, Ayrton takes his third stint after only two short hours of sleep. The advice given by Dalmas and Sekiya is starting to pay off. Without reducing his pace, he now achieves fuel consumption levels similar to his teammates. In the last half-hour, he even manages to slightly outperform them. The triple world champion learns quickly when it comes to chasing victory.

After a shower and a hearty breakfast, he returns to the pit. He has two more hours of driving starting at noon, but at this point, fatigue begins to set in. His neck is stiff, and a slight pain tugs at his forearms. However, too proud to acknowledge what he considers a weakness, he keeps it to himself and continues his work discussions with the team personnel.

For the last time of the weekend, he takes over from Yannick Dalmas at noon, and Masanori Sekiya will then be responsible for completing these 24 hours of testing. Around 1:00 p.m., the Lanzante team is surprised not to see the black McLaren zooming down the straight when, nearly a minute later, the GT appears slowly in the pit lane. Judging by the marks on the hood, the car has likely had a minor off-track excursion. Stationed in front of the garage, the door opens. Senna unbuckles his harness and gets out of the car. Yet, he still has almost an hour of driving left to complete. Paul Lanzante, accompanied by two engineers, rushes over to question the Brazilian:

-   What's happening, Ayrton?

-   I'm suffering from terrible forearm cramps.
    When I tried to correct oversteer during the
    acceleration at Campbell Corner, I couldn't
    and spun out. The front hit the tire wall, but
    the impact was minor. I'm sorry, but I think
    it's best if I stop for today.

-   No problem, we'll have Masanori take over to
    finish the simulation.

-   I feel terrible about it. I've neglected my
    physical preparation for the past year. I still
    have two months to make it right.

Upset by this withdrawal, the driver bids farewell to
his interlocutors and heads to Nuno Cobra, his
physical trainer. During his Formula 1 years, this
graduate from the University of Sao Paulo
accompanied him throughout the season. Ayrton, not
particularly interested in physical effort, has
sometimes finished Grand Prix races on the brink of
exhaustion due to insufficient training. Thanks to
Nuno, he had become disciplined in this area,
considering it essential to his success. Since his
retirement, he has let go and is paying the price this
Sunday. But with the goal of the 24 Hours of Le
Mans in mind, he leaves Thruxton determined to
resume serious training with Nuno.

Angra dos Reis, Friday, May 12, 1995

Comfortably seated by the poolside of his gigantic Brazilian estate, Ayrton Senna indulges in a moment of relaxation after the rigorous workout session he just put himself through: a 10-kilometer run, followed by an hour of weightlifting, and ending with 30 minutes of stretching. Since the unfortunate incident at Thruxton, he has regained his former Formula 1 driver's physical condition through rigorous daily training and a more nutritious diet.

Adriane, returning from yet another trip abroad for her modeling career, is by his side. Although they haven't seen each other for several weeks, Ayrton doesn't seem as thrilled to see her as usual. Just a few minutes after her arrival at the house, he once again reproached her about her closeness to an assistant employed by her modeling agency. The young man is responsible for organizing Adriane's schedule during her travels and consequently spends a lot of time with her. To Ayrton's eyes, far too much time. However, their relationship is purely professional, but Ayrton has shown extreme jealousy towards her on more than one occasion. Hadn't he paid a hefty sum to buy back revealing photos of her to prevent them from being published again in the press, as was the case at the beginning of their relationship?

Up until now, Adriane had been patient and had accepted, more or less, this flaw that seemed to affect many men. But on that day, the young model is much less forgiving than usual when the scenes of jealousy with Ayrton erupt. Silent, she remains seated on the edge of the pool. Behind her sunglasses, she tries to hold back her tears. Her body trembles slightly. She is on the verge of a nervous breakdown. This time, Ayrton has gone too far by doubting her loyalty. The closeness with her companion bothers her, and she finally decides to retreat and isolate herself in their room.

In his sun lounger, the Brazilian is engrossed in reading a magazine and seems oblivious to Adriane's state of nervousness. He will quickly learn about it when he sees her reappear, dragging a huge suitcase behind her.

-   Ayrton, I think it's no longer possible for us. Your jealousy has become unbearable for me. You constantly reproach me for imaginary behaviors, and I'm at my wit's end. I believe it's better for me to leave, she says, her words cutting through the silence and tranquility of the place.

Dumbfounded by what he has just heard, Senna struggles to find his words. While he had noticed that Adriane was upset, he didn't realize he had hurt her to this extent. However, considering his reproaches legitimate and too proud to admit his mistake, his response does nothing to ease the situation.

- Listen, Adriane, I think your trip has exhausted you. You don't know what you're saying anymore. You'd better go upstairs and rest, and we'll talk about all this when you've calmed down.

- You don't understand anything, Ayrton. This time, I'm leaving. I called a taxi. It's waiting for me at the entrance of the property.

Thinking that his fiancée would seek refuge with a friend or her parents, Ayrton decides to leave it at that for today. She seemed too angry for him to try to dissuade her. After all, after a few days of reflection, she would surely come back, and everything would return to normal.

However, at that moment, Ayrton Senna is unaware that Adriane will not return, and he will never have any contact with her again after this dramatic departure. Exactly one year after his abrupt retirement from Formula 1, this breakup would once again disrupt the life of the Brazilian champion.

Le Mans, Saturday, June 17, 1995

It's the big day. In a few minutes, Ayrton Senna will take the start of his first 24 Hours of Le Mans. Given his extraordinary attacking abilities, he has been designated to drive the McLaren No. 59 as the first driver. The team hopes that he will be able to position himself immediately at the front and thus minimize the risk of collision. During the practice sessions, he had already proven to be the fastest among the six entered McLaren F1 cars. With a time of 3'56"76, he places his car in ninth position on the starting grid, behind a few untouchable prototypes and the swift Ferrari F40s.

Since his arrival in Sarthe, he has been literally harassed by journalists. This is his first car competition in over a year, and commentators have thousands of questions to ask him. A few minutes before the start of the race, he isolates himself in the cockpit of his GT. Although he no longer felt this way when he raced in F1, nervousness begins to invade him. The media pressure and the unknowns of a new discipline are likely the cause. In the eyes of the general public, he is one of the favorites for these 24 hours, but despite being completely confident in his abilities as a driver, he knows that he is still a rookie, albeit a prestigious one. His mishap during the simulation is etched in his memory and proves the difficulty of this challenge.

Stripped of mechanics and accredited observers, the starting grid is left to the competitors. At 3:55 PM, the race officials initiate the warm-up lap, after which the race will begin with a rolling start. As they pass under the green flag, the WR and Courage cars surge ahead. Their lap pace is significantly faster than that of the GT cars, but the regulations penalize them in terms of fuel consumption, and they will have to refuel more frequently during the 24 hours.

Following the recommendations of his team, Senna has been cautious and managed to navigate through the pack without incident. After a few laps, he is even overtaken by two McLarens, the No. 49 "West" and the No. 51 "Harrod's," and he obediently stays behind, adhering to the pre-established race plan.

After only 45 minutes of racing, the arrival of rain disrupts the hierarchy. At the end of the first hour, car No. 49 is leading ahead of car No. 51, while "Pesca" holds the third position after a very conservative start to the race. Senna, for his part, is navigating in eighth position, but the wet conditions will highlight his formidable driving skills.

Shortly after, Ray Bellm goes off track and damages the front of his McLaren No. 24. He has to return to the pit for repairs. Senna thus gains one position.

On the weather front, rain has decided to settle in at the Circuit du Mans, causing numerous spins and off-track incidents. Around 7 PM, Patrick Gonin hydroplanes at high speed on the Mulsanne Straight.

The impact is severe, rendering the driver of car No. 8, a WR, unconscious. The race is neutralized, and the safety car is deployed to allow rescue workers to attend to the unfortunate driver. Ayrton Senna watches all of this from the pit as he has handed over the wheel to Masanori Sekiya. Although he was aware of the risks, this major crash serves as a reminder that this race can be particularly dangerous, especially in the rain, at night, and while navigating through slower backmarker drivers.

During the hour-long neutralization, two serious contenders encounter mechanical issues. Franck Lagorce, who took over from Pescarolo in the Courage, unsuccessfully attempts to push his stalled car at the Arnage corner. As for McLaren No. 51, the problem with the clutch cable costs them their second position, allowing the Courage-Porsche of the Wollek-Hélary-Andretti crew to move up. Behind the wheel of this prototype marked with the usually avoided No. 13, Mario Andretti, 55 years old, aims to add the prestigious Le Mans victory to his already illustrious career, which includes Formula 1 (1978 World Champion) and CART, the American open-wheel championship.

From garage, Senna doesn't miss a single moment of his teammate's progress, who currently holds fifth place, two laps behind McLaren No. 49. But just as he is being signaled by his engineer to go for a massage in preparation for his second stint, he spots the Courage C34 in distress on the grass. Mario Andretti, while approaching the Ford chicanes, was caught off guard by a slower backmarker and lost control of his prototype, hitting the wall from the rear. With a broken wing and suspension, the driver immediately returns to the track to bring his damaged car back to the French team's pit. For 25 long minutes, the mechanics work diligently to repair the machine. It will be able to continue, but with several laps behind.

At 9 PM, with Yannick Dalmas now behind the wheel of car No. 59, the provisional podium is still dominated by McLaren No. 49, 25, and 51. Dalmas is in fifth position but has closed the gap to one lap behind the leader. He quickly gains another position when Spanish driver Pareja crashes his Porsche GT1 into the wall at the same spot where Andretti went off. Pareja was partnering with Jean-Pierre Jarier and Erik Comas, both former Formula 1 drivers.

Sitting in his motorhome, Senna enjoys a snack with Sekiya. The Japanese driver, participating in his ninth Le Mans, explains to him that those who will win this edition are those who make the fewest mistakes. As night falls over the Sarthe, the unfolding events seem to confirm his statement.

In his racing suit, Senna makes his appearance in the pit just before 11 PM. He is about to begin his first night stint. As Dalmas appears in the pit lane, he has just moved up to third place following the retirement of the Raphanel-Alliot-Owen-Jones McLaren. Senna informs him of this news as he helps him out of the cockpit. Equipped with four new tires and a full fuel tank, the Brazilian plunges into the darkness of the rain-soaked Sarthe circuit.

In these conditions, his driving skills are exceptional.

He has retained from his British Formula 3 years an extraordinary ability to drive on wet tracks. Closing in at a rate of two seconds per lap, he is catching up to the No. 51 driven by Andy Wallace, Dereck Bell, and Justin Bell. Dereck is a legend of the 24 Hours of Le Mans, having already won the race five times. This year, at nearly 54 years old, he is aiming for a sixth victory, partnering with his son Justin.

Observing the pace of his driver, the race engineer is both amazed and filled with worry. Will Senna be able to maintain this rhythm without making any mistakes? Inside the McLaren, he feels particularly comfortable. He overtakes backmarkers one after another and gains more and more confidence. Delaying his braking a bit here, accelerating earlier there, he pushes the limits of his machine lap after lap.

On the 98th lap, he catches up to a Venturi just before the braking point of the first chicane on the Mulsanne Straight. Wanting to pass it before the deceleration, he positions himself on the inside to overtake just before the braking point. Slightly off the ideal racing line by a few centimeters, he presses the brake pedal as his left front wheel passes over a puddle of water. Suddenly destabilized, his McLaren spins in an impressive series of spins before coming to a stop in the runoff area. Fortunately, the out-of-control car encounters no obstacles during its wild ride and comes to rest on a paved section. Senna only needs to engage first gear to rejoin the track and continue his stint.

Having recovered from the incident, this off-track

excursion brings back the memory of one of Senna's biggest disappointments as a driver. It was during the 1988 Monaco Grand Prix. Leading the race with over 50 seconds ahead of Alain Prost and only 12 laps remaining, he could have eased off and secured the victory. However, that day, fueled by both overconfidence and a desire to humiliate his teammate, he continued to push and ultimately lost the race after a foolish mistake in the Portier corner. Furious with himself, he had walked straight back to his Monaco apartment to digest his disappointment alone.

Not wanting to relive that negative experience, he makes the decision to reduce his pace a bit. With nearly 15 hours of racing left, the checkered flag is still far away. Sekiya was right, he thinks to himself. This will be a race of attrition. It's best to avoid being among the casualties.

After a much more cautious end to his stint, he hands over the wheel to Sekiya around 1:30 AM. It's time for him to get some sleep before getting back in the cockpit in the early morning.

When his alarm clock rings, he can see the daylight through the windows of his motorhome. Quickly drinking a cup of coffee, he does some warm-up exercises to wake up his body and mind because Yannick Dalmas will soon hand over the car to him.

As soon as he returns to the pit, he rushes to check the race standings and realizes that their car is now in second position. The No. 49 McLaren, which had been leading for several hours, suffered an off-track excursion and then had to retire shortly after 3 AM when its clutch failed. Now, they have to chase down the "Harrod's" crew of Wallace-Bell-Bell while also keeping an eye on the incredible comeback of the No. 13 Courage, which is in third place despite its long pit stop at the beginning of the race.

As the track conditions improve with the rain subsiding, Senna regains his confidence to attack again, sensing that he can catch up to the No. 51 McLaren. Despite Justin Bell's best efforts, the Brazilian inexorably closes in on his prey. After two hours of relentless pursuit, the gap is reduced to just 30 seconds. Not wanting to break this momentum, the team director at Lanzante requests Senna to extend his stint over the radio.

Shortly before 9 AM, Senna has closed in on the leader's rear, but fatigue is starting to take its toll. He has been driving for over three hours non-stop and doesn't want to repeat his mistake at Thruxton. With a heavy heart, as his instincts urge him to continue and attempt an attack, he requests to come into the pits through the radio. Yannick Dalmas is then sent back out on track as he is deemed faster than Sekiya in order to take the lead. In just a few laps, the Frenchman catches up to the front-running car and launches an initial attack. Hindered by a backmarker, he patiently tucks in behind it before making another move in the Hunaudières. This second attempt is successful, and car No. 59 takes the lead amid the cheers from the Lanzante team.

Exhausted and suffering from muscle cramps, Ayrton

Senna settles on the massage table. As his physiotherapist works on his muscles, he quickly drifts off to sleep, filled with dreams of victory.

Behind the wheel of their respective McLarens, Dalmas and Wallace constantly exchange the lead as they go through their pit stops and refueling. However, as Dalmas nears the end of his stint, he complains of a problem with his left front brake. Upon returning to the pits, the mechanics rush to address the issue, but despite their efficiency, the No. 51 car manages to create some breathing space. It's back to square one!

Now, all hopes of the team rest on Masanori Sekiya. With a fully operational braking system, he can once again push and gradually close the gap to Andy Wallace. The pace of the British driver keeps dropping. As he passes by the pits, the Lanzante mechanics detect a gearbox issue. The information is immediately relayed to Sekiya, who regains hope for a victory.

When he hands over the car to Dalmas, the designated driver to take the checkered flag, Sekiya has closed the gap to the leaders to around 40 seconds, as they struggle more and more with their gearbox. During his final pit stop, Dereck Bell faces considerable difficulty engaging first gear. Eventually, he succeeds, but the pit stop has taken over a minute and forty seconds. With just half an hour remaining, he helplessly sees the black McLaren closing in through his rearview mirrors. Yannick Dalmas swiftly overtakes and regains the lead. Now, all he has to do is hold on and pray to be spared from any technical issues. On the pit wall, Senna and Sekiya support each other, not missing a moment of their teammate's progress.

15:55. The No. 59 car begins its final lap before the end of the 24-hour race. The driver even has to slow down to avoid crossing the finish line before 16:00, thus preventing an additional lap of the entire circuit. He can afford to do so because the No. 13 Courage, which managed to overtake the ailing No. 51 McLaren, is over 3 minutes behind.

At a slow speed, the black machine, covered in oil and mud, enters the chicane of the connecting road. It overtakes a final backmarker who graciously moves aside to not steal the spotlight on the photo finish. With one last acceleration, it triumphantly passes under the checkered flag. The driver opens his door and greets his team and two co-drivers, who embrace him in celebration.

Surrounded by a swarm of journalists, Dalmas parks the McLaren in the parc fermé. Senna and Sekiya have already joined him and lift him up in triumph. The image will make the front page of many sports newspapers the next day. Now, it's time for the podium ceremony, as the tradition goes, while the public has already flooded the track.

Andy Wallace and the Bell father-and-son duo are the first to step onto the podium. Despite their gearbox troubles, they managed to salvage third place, but disappointment is evident on their faces despite the obligatory smiles. Eric Hélary, Mario Andretti, and

Bob Wollek quickly join them. Did the winner of the 1993 edition have a chance to win alongside the greatest bad luck charm at Le Mans, and in a car bearing the number 13? Indeed, in 25 participations at the wheel of the most high-performance cars, Alsatian driver Bob Wollek secures his fourth podium in Le Mans without ever experiencing the joys of victory. His young compatriot, on the other hand, won in 1993 behind the wheel of the formidable Peugeot 905 in his very first participation. As for Mario Andretti, he regrets making the mistake at the beginning of the race that cost them an indisputable triumph. But the fifty-year-old has already promised to return next year.

Finally, the trio of winners appears, receiving their crowns of flowers. Senna and Sekiya flank Yannick Dalmas on the highest step of the podium. While it is a first for the two men, the Frenchman raises his third trophy in four editions. At 34 years old, he is becoming a legend of the 24 hours, and the crowd recognizes it by loudly applauding him. Senna, who still can't believe he managed to win the greatest endurance race in the world, is overwhelmed by emotion, amplified by fatigue. During the national anthems, the cameras focused on him capture a few tears that he struggles to contain.

Laughter fills the air as the champagne ceremony concludes, and the three winners make their way to the press room for another marathon, this time with the media. But to their surprise, at the bottom of the stairs, they spot a gleeful Ron Dennis personally congratulating them. The McLaren boss hadn't planned to attend the race, but the likely victory of one of his cars, and let's admit it, his beloved driver, prompted him to jump aboard his private plane bound for Le Mans.

Embracing Dalmas and Sekiya while offering his congratulations, he lingers a bit longer with Ayrton, exchanging a few words.

-   You see, Ayrton, I told you the story would be great!

-   Ron... Be honest... Did you really believe in this victory when you proposed that I be part of the adventure?

-   Maybe not as much as I sold it to you, but it was a possibility I considered.

-   Because if I look at the standings; without their half-hour pit stop, the Courage would have easily put us 5 or 6 laps behind.

-   That's endurance, Ayrton. It's not always the fastest that prevails.

-   That's precisely what I reproach it for! Senna retorts, bursting into laughter.

Buenos Aires, Saturday, July 15, 1995

Upon learning that the great Juan-Manuel Fangio was hospitalized with a severe pneumonia, Ayrton didn't hesitate for a second. The doctors had little hope for the recovery of the Argentine. His days were numbered. Wanting to see his illustrious predecessor one last time, he immediately boarded his private plane bound for Buenos Aires.

With a heavy heart, he passed through the hospital doors. Recognizing him despite his attempt to go incognito, a few fans rushed towards him seeking a handshake and an autograph. Politely, the Brazilian obliged but cut the encounter short, explaining that it wasn't the right time or place for it. That's when a department head took charge and escorted him to room number 319.

Entering the dimly lit room, Ayrton, being a highly sensitive person, felt his legs weaken. Fangio lay on the bed with his eyes closed. He was intubated and supported by a ventilator. Under the influence of sedatives administered by the doctors, he seemed to be peacefully asleep. Ayrton circled the bed and took a seat on the chair placed beside the patient's bed. The old man still hadn't realized the presence of this unexpected visitor by his side. For several minutes, only the mechanics of the ventilator broke the silence of the room. Ayrton, too, closed his eyes and prayed for the man he admired so much.

Nearly half a century separates them, but the two champions have always been very close since Ayrton's arrival in Formula 1. Both South Americans with Italian origins, they have each left an indelible mark in their sport. Born on June 24, 1911, in Balcarce, Juan-Manuel Fangio developed a passion for mechanics at an early age, becoming an apprentice at the age of 11. It was only at the age of 25 that he participated in his first race behind the wheel of a Ford A. Thanks to his exceptional abilities, he gradually made a name for himself in the Argentinean motorsport scene. The Second World War temporarily interrupted his momentum before the rise to power of General Peron, a great racing enthusiast, propelled him onto the international stage. Competing with the best European drivers who came to participate in the temporadas organized during the southern summer by the Argentinean president's initiative, he was later sent to Europe by the automobile club of his country starting from 1948. In the old continent, he took part in his first Grand Prix in Reims, replacing the injured Maurice Trintignant in an accident during a race held in Switzerland. His Simca-Gordini did not allow him to compete with the powerful Alfettas, and he was forced to retire due to an engine failure. The following year, the Argentinean automobile club provided him with a Maserati 4CLT, with which he would rack up victories. At the age of 38, his Grand Prix career was finally launched.

Starting in 1950, the Formula 1 World Championship was created. Until 1958, the year of his retirement, he would win nearly one out of every two races and secure five world championships with four different manufacturers. Four decades later, as he experienced his final moments in that Buenos Aires hospital, no other driver had surpassed his achievements, and the Great Fangio had become a legend.

Crossing paths on the circuits several times, the two champions had forged strong bonds. Fangio regarded Senna as his worthy heir and almost like a son. Ayrton, in turn, held immense admiration for this extraordinary man. A gentleman on the track, Fangio had managed to build an exceptional record while earning the respect of his rivals. But unlike many of them who were killed behind the wheel of their cars, he would die as an octogenarian in a bed.

As he prepares to leave the room, Ayrton takes the old man's hand to bid him farewell. That's when he sees his eyelids partially open, revealing the piercing blue of his eyes. Unable to speak due to the tube inserted in his throat, Fangio tightens his grip on his visitor's fingers with the last strength he has left. Despite the effects of the medication, he has recognized him well, and his presence seems to bring him some comfort. Locking eyes with the Brazilian for a few seconds, he cannot prevent his eyelids from slowly closing. Fangio is much too weak, and Ayrton decides to let him rest. Before taking his leave, his throat choked up, he whispers in his ear, "May you have a peaceful journey, Mr. Fangio," then slowly exits the room to head to the airport where his plane awaits.

48 hours later, he will learn that Fangio succumbed to a final heart attack. He was 84 years old.

São Paulo, Monday, February 26, 1996

In the Senna family, there is the father, Milton da Silva, married to Neide Senna. From this union, three children were born: Viviane in 1958, Ayrton in 1960, and Leonardo in 1966. Married to Flavio Lalli, Viviane gave birth to two children: Bruno in 1983 and Bianca the following year. Ayrton himself, without children, has always been very close to his nephew and niece. While he was still active, he would invite them to spend vacations in Angra dos Reis whenever his schedule allowed it. In his vast farm, he had built a karting track in Tatui. It was on this ribbon of asphalt that he introduced young Bruno to the joys of racing when he was only six years old.

Fascinated by his uncle's profession, Bruno would train in karting whenever he had the opportunity. In the summer of 1991, Ayrton organized a race for children. It would be Bruno's first victory in competition. Year after year, Bruno would wear out the seat of his kart, trying to apply the precious advice of his uncle. It seems that talent runs in the family because in the summer of 1993, at not even 10 years old, he set the absolute record for the Tatui track. Speaking of him in the media, Ayrton declared, "If you think I'm good, wait until you see my nephew Bruno."

Although one can doubt the objectivity of an uncle about his beloved nephew, the compliment came from a triple Formula 1 world champion nonetheless.

Since his retirement from the sport, Ayrton dedicates much more time to his loved ones, especially Bruno, with whom he shares the same passion for speed. At twelve years old, Bruno is now licensed in the cadet category and regularly participates in regional races.

Although concerned about the dangers of motorsport, his parents Flavio and Viviane have complete trust in Ayrton to provide him with the best advice. Flavio is also a lover of fine machinery, particularly motorcycles. When he had entered into a partnership with the Italian manufacturer Ducati to use his name, Ayrton surprised and moved his brother-in-law by giving him a 916 in 1995 for his 37th birthday. It was the most sporty motorcycle in the lineup, and he had even contributed to its development by becoming a luxury test rider for the brand.

This Monday morning, Flavio mounts his steed to go to his office in the heart of Sao Paulo's business district. In this gigantic metropolis, traffic flows in a "South American" way, which means rather anarchic and disorganized. After a few minutes of travel, Bruno's father enters a highway. At this time of the day, the traffic is particularly dense, and Flavio navigates his way through the countless taxis. Suddenly, one of them changes lanes without warning, right in front of the wheels of the red motorcycle. The collision is unavoidable, and the

Ducati is violently thrown to the ground with its rider. The needle of his watch, broken in the impact, stopped at 8:27. At 38 years old, Flavio Lalli has ceased to live.

His funeral takes place four days later at the Morumbi cemetery, an oasis of greenery amidst the skyscrapers of the bustling city of São Paulo. Deeply affected by the tragic and sudden loss of his brother-in-law, Ayrton has not left Viviane and her children since he heard the news.

He is particularly distressed because he feels a strong sense of guilt about what has just happened. Wasn't it him who put this red missile in Flavio's hands, which was ultimately ill-suited for urban traffic? Viviane quickly absolved him of any responsibility, believing that fate had placed that taxi in her husband's path.

A few days after the ceremony, Ayrton returned alone to pay his respects at Flavio's grave. He prayed for the salvation of his soul for a long time and, before leaving, promised to watch over Viviane and the children. Already very close to them, this tragedy will further strengthen his bonds with Bianca and Bruno.

Tatui Karting Track, Thursday, July 18, 1996

Five months after the death of his father, Bruno Lalli finds himself at his uncle's place in Angra Dos Reis. As he has done since his early childhood, he has come to spend a few days with Ayrton during the break between the two semesters of the school year in Brazil.

On board his kart, he follows the champion who has also taken to the track. Despite having a less powerful machine than Ayrton's, the young boy follows him thanks to his lighter weight. With determination, he corrects his vehicle's trajectory with vigorous steering movements.

Although it is just a simple two-person ride, the competitive instinct of the three-time world champion pushes him to increase his pace. Unable to keep up on the straightaways, Bruno tries to make up for lost ground in the twisty sections. Lap after lap, he pushes his braking points further to gain a few hundredths of a second. Surprised to see him still so close, Ayrton adjusts the richness of his fuel mixture to seek a few extra power, realizing that he can no longer gain much in terms of pure driving skills. Bruno takes note of the scene and adjusts the dial on his carburetor accordingly.

At the limit of a spin-out during the circuit's heaviest braking zone, Ayrton avoids going off track with a magnificent countersteer but loses a few tenths of a second in the process. Bruno is now only a few centimeters behind his elder's kart, but Ayrton gains some breathing room in the following straightaway. Undeterred, at the next braking point, Bruno attempts an attack from the inside of the racing line. Being a seasoned circuit veteran, Ayrton graciously opens the door by staying wide on the outside, knowing that his nephew, carried away by his speed, will not be able to take the ideal racing line. As expected, the teenager exits the corner too wide, and Ayrton, able to accelerate earlier, regains the advantage.

Despite his youth and inexperience, Bruno has learned his lesson, and when he finds himself in a position to attack once again a lap later, he pretends to attempt the same maneuver from the inside. Instinctively, Ayrton defends his position by also steering slightly towards the inside while leaving enough space to maintain the hope of overtaking him. But unexpectedly, he suddenly steers his kart towards the outside at the braking point. Now, it is Bruno who has the better racing line and can accelerate earlier. Side by side with his uncle, on the next straight, he finds himself on the right side of the track for the upcoming right turn. Being on the inside of the track, he has a shorter distance to cover while Ayrton continues to resist on his left. As the corner tightens, he pushes his rival to touch the curbs. The only option left for Ayrton is to concede if he doesn't want to end up in the grass. In this exercise, the student has surpassed the master.

Back at the pit, Bruno throws himself into Ayrton's arms. Since the death of his father, he hadn't experienced such joy. By battling against his family idol, he has had a revelation. He also wants to live the life of a Grand Prix driver, and he is counting on Ayrton to help him achieve his goal.

Montreal, Gilles Villeneuve Circuit
Monday, June 16, 1997

Returning from the Sacré-Cœur Hospital in Montreal, Alain Prost's cellphone rang. On the other end of the line, he immediately recognized Ayrton's voice. His former teammate had already called him the previous evening to inquire about Olivier Panis, who had suffered a serious accident during the Canadian Grand Prix. After hitting a curb, the Grenoble native felt that a mechanical component had failed. While accelerating, he suddenly lost control of his Prost-Mugen Honda. The car bounced off the wall before crashing into a stack of tires. In the impact, Panis believed he could hear the bones in his legs breaking. X-rays confirmed his grim premonition. Operated on that evening, the Frenchman was about to begin a long period of recovery that would keep him away from the racetracks.

This accident couldn't have come at a worse time for Panis, whose career was starting to take off. Having won the epic Monaco Grand Prix the previous year, he was in third place in the championship upon arriving in Montreal. Only Jacques Villeneuve and Michael Schumacher were ahead of him. After finishing fifth in the opening race in Melbourne, he had secured a podium finish in third place at Interlagos. Betrayed by his machinery in Argentina after starting in third position, he had ended up outside the points in Imola. Then, one year after his Monaco triumph, he had claimed fourth place in the rain-soaked Monaco Grand Prix once again, followed by another podium finish in Barcelona behind Villeneuve and ahead of Jean Alesi. His Ligier-designed Prost JS 45 was well born, and his V10 Mugen-Honda engine was performing strongly. Under these circumstances, he was having by far his best Formula 1 season. Unfortunately, this momentum came to an abrupt end against the tire wall at the Gilles Villeneuve circuit.

Sitting in the living room of his luxurious Portuguese villa, Ayrton is reassured by the new team manager about the progress of his injured driver's health.

- The operation went well. We had to insert pins to align his fractures. His season is probably over, but he should be able to race again, explains the native of Saint-Chamond, still in shock.

- What a stroke of bad luck. His start to the season had impressed me, says Ayrton.

- It seems like it was too good to be true, Prost replies somewhat fatalistically.

- The important thing is that he is out of danger, although I suppose a new team like yours didn't need this, remarks Ayrton.

- I couldn't agree more, Ayrton, Prost nods,

Now we need to find a solution for Magny-Cours, and it's our home Grand Prix!

- Do you have any leads? I imagine your phone must have been ringing off the hook in the past few hours.

- Talented young drivers are not lacking, but a new team like ours also needs experience to progress. I won't hide from you that I'm pondering a lot. I can't afford to make a mistake.

- That's not good news for your nails!, the Brazilian replies, trying to lighten the mood.

- It's the tough apprenticeship of a team manager.

- You know, Alain, I might be able to help you this time.

- Oh really? Have you embarked on a career as a driver's agent? Prost asks, half amused and half intrigued.

- In a way, Senna replies enigmatically.

- So, who do you recommend? Prost continues, growing more and more curious.

- He's a Brazilian who's no longer young but still has a great driving skill and solid experience in the sport. And to give you another argument in his favor, he has already won the World Championship three times!

- Are you kidding, Ayrton! exclaims the Frenchman, unsure if he should take this unexpected and tempting proposal seriously.

- Absolutely not, Alain. I couldn't be more serious at this moment.

- Well, you leave me speechless. It's been three years since you retired.

- That's precisely why I'm starting to feel restless and miss the competition. And I'm only 37 years old. I've been considering a comeback for a while now. This abrupt retirement left me with a sense of unfinished business. Lauda also stopped for three years before getting back behind the wheel and even won another title in '84. You know that as well as I do.

- I don't doubt your abilities. I'm just surprised by your proposal. I thought you had moved on, but if that's what you want, I can only approve. Can you imagine the media impact of such an announcement?

- Surely, Senna returning to competition, especially driving for Prost, will create a buzz! But first and foremost, I want to make it clear that no matter what happens, I will give Panis his seat back once he's recovered.

- And how do you see your future beyond this temporary stint?

- I don't know. One step at a time. I just want to regain my sensations, and we'll see after a few races.

- With what you just told me, we need to meet at the factory as soon as possible. I plan to take the plane tonight.

- Okay, I'll be at Magny-Cours on Wednesday morning without fail.

This new offer gives Alain Prost a moment of respite in the ordeal that has struck his team. Deeming his injured driver still too weak hours after his operation, he decides to wait a bit before announcing the identity of his replacement to the injured driver. He will call him before sharing the information with the press and assure him that he will regain his place as soon as his physical condition allows. Now, he needs to go and pick up Anne Panis at the airport. Olivier's wife hastily boarded the first plane to Canada to be by his side.

Circuit de Nevers-Magny-Cours, Friday, June 27, 1997

As planned, the announcement of Ayrton Senna's recruitment to replace Olivier Panis in Prost Racing caused a sensation in the F1 community. Within hours, the remaining tickets for the French Grand Prix were sold at exorbitant prices. Every fan wanted to be there to witness the return of "Magic" Senna, as journalist Johnny Rives had nicknamed him in L'Equipe.

After visiting the factory to have his seat molded, the Brazilian driver acquainted himself with his new team. It was as if he had never left the sport, quickly settling back into his work routine.

On this Friday morning, there was an air of excitement around Prost's garage, labeled as number 14. Just moments before the first free practice session, Ayrton secluded himself in a corner of the pit. Already wearing his helmet, he appeared contemplative. The dozens of photographers present wondered what he might be thinking, eager to capture this moment. Perhaps he was experiencing some nervousness, like an artist before stepping onto the stage. Maybe he doubted the wisdom of his decision now that he was backed into a corner. He couldn't turn back anymore. To prevent himself from overthinking, he settled into the cockpit of his blue single-seater very early on. He was eager to get going. Even though the light was still red, he was the first one to emerge from the pit lane. After two installation laps, during which he familiarized himself with the functioning of his steering wheel under real conditions, he gradually increased his pace. After completing his first run of eight laps, he returned to the pits feeling completely reassured. The car provided him with good sensations. He felt comfortable enough to push despite not having fine-tuned the settings yet. However, the wet track conditions he encountered that morning added an extra challenge to his Prost learning experience. Instead of unsettling him, the rain brought back fond memories of his past career. It was under pouring rain that he had achieved some of his most remarkable feats.

In 1984, when he debuted in F1 for the modest Toleman team, he narrowly missed victory in Monaco, losing to Alain Prost, who was already a formidable competitor. Surging forward, closing in on the leading McLaren, his momentum was abruptly halted by the checkered flag being waved before completing the scheduled 78 laps for safety reasons. He had overtaken Prost a few seconds prior, but the official classification was determined based on the previous lap, as specified by the regulations. Ayrton had felt a deep sense of injustice in that moment.

Despite that setback, the performances of the young Brazilian rookie had not gone unnoticed, and he was recruited by the prestigious Lotus-Renault team for the 1985 season. In only his second Grand Prix at Estoril in Portugal, he stood out by securing the first of his 65 pole positions. In the race, under heavy rain, he executed a splendid solo performance, leaving all his competitors a lap behind, with Alboreto being the only exception, finishing second over a minute behind the winner.

He also vividly remembered the famous 1993 Donington Grand Prix. On that day, he had simply humiliated Alain Prost in a McLaren-Ford that was clearly inferior to the Williams-Renault of the "Professor." However, the technical inferiority had been overshadowed by the brilliance of the driver in the rain.

Ayrton didn't hesitate to playfully remind his new boss of that episode during the dinner shared with the team members at the end of that first day of testing.

Circuit de Nevers-Magny-Cours, Saturday, June 28, 1997

The sun had returned to the Nevers region as the qualifying session for the French Grand Prix began. This would be the ultimate test for Ayrton, who excelled in the pure speed exercise. Sitting on the edge of the pit wall, Alain Prost and Cesare Fiorio, the team's sporting director, were just as tense as their illustrious recruit. This afternoon, the Brazilians were the quickest to take to the track. Behind the wheel of his Stewart-Ford, Rubens Barrichello set the first benchmark time: 1'16.059. Ayrton followed closely behind. In his first fast lap, he clocked an impressive 1'15.317. He had already beaten last year's pole position time by almost seven-tenths of a second. On his return to the pit lane, he immediately gave instructions over the radio. He wanted to slightly adjust the brake balance between the front and rear. He had nearly been caught off guard at the entry of the Lycée hairpin, the final corner of the track. Without that moment, he believed he could have done better. In any case, as more cars went through, the track would gradually rubber in, improving grip and therefore performance.

Ayrton Senna had just enough time to enter his team's box and see that his time had been beaten by Jean Alesi's Benetton, with a lap time of 1'15.250.

However, the Frenchman's provisional pole position would only last a few seconds before his teammate, Alexander Wurz, did slightly better by just 19 milliseconds. This 22-year-old Austrian was only in his second Formula 1 Grand Prix. He had replaced Gerhard Berger, Ayrton's regular teammate and friend, since the Canadian round. Berger had been dealing with a persistent sinus infection, undergoing several operations, and was expected to make his comeback at Hockenheim at the end of July.

As Wurz completed his slow-down lap, the Ferrari of Michael Schumacher suddenly appeared, accelerating in front of the pits. The German, a two-time world champion, was the defending champion at Magny-Cours. Needless to say, he was a serious contender for pole position. Despite a wheel lock-up and a slight loss of grip in the final chicane, "Schumi" smashed Wurz's time by nearly seven-tenths of a second, setting a time of 1'14.548.

" It will be difficult to do better," Ayrton thought as he looked at the screen placed in front of the windshield of his Prost. The following minutes seemed to prove the Brazilian right. Behind the wheel of the Williams-Renault, Heinz-Harald Frentzen crossed the line in 1'15.008. Although his car was still considered the best on the grid and had already won four races in the hands of both Frentzen and Jacques Villeneuve, another driver would also break the 1'15" barrier, giving hope to Schumacher's rivals. It was Ralf Schumacher, the younger brother of Michael, who had been driving a Jordan powered by a Peugeot V10 since the beginning of the season. His time of

1'14.755 put him just two-tenths behind his older brother, but his car was neither a Williams nor a Ferrari, making his achievement even more impressive. It should be remembered that Ralf, who would turn 22 in two days, was participating in only his eighth Formula 1 testing session at Magny-Cours. In the previous seven, he had always qualified in the top 10, except for his first Grand Prix in Melbourne.

Continuously observing his opponents on his control screen, Ayrton noticed that many drivers were quicker in the first sector before falling behind in the two more twisty sections of the track. Schumacher had prioritized handling over top speed, and it was paying off for him. Ayrton decided to adjust his rear wing angle, aiming to improve both the balance of his car, which he felt was too oversteery, and his straight-line speed. With the adjustment made, he lowered his visor and set off to attack the chronometer once again.

He passed the first intermediate point with a two-tenths deficit to the German. His customer Mugen Honda engine wasn't as powerful as the Ferrari V10. After navigating the Adelaide hairpin flawlessly, he sped towards the Nürburgring chicane before approaching the "180-degree" corner, where he believed his adjusted wing could gain him some time. At the second intermediate, he managed to maintain his gap to the Ferrari. Only the Château d'Eau corner and the challenging sequence leading to the Lycée hairpin remained for him to complete his lap. As he crossed the finish line, he glimpsed at his time on the screen: 1'14.752. By a mere three-thousandths of a second, he managed to slot himself into second position, sandwiched between the Schumacher brothers. Prost and Fiorio exchanged a satisfied handshake in the pit lane.

In a second attempt, Michael Schumacher failed to improve but still set the second-best time of the afternoon. There was still fifteen minutes remaining before the checkered flag. Ayrton returned to the pits, closely following Frentzen's lap on his screen. The German was very close to him after the second sector. When his time appeared, Ayrton couldn't help but express his disappointment, pounding his fist on the steering wheel. He was beaten by a mere three-thousandths of a second! Having witnessed the scene, Prost leaned in and whispered into Cesare Fiorio's ear, "He hasn't changed!" His face adorned with a broad smile.

As the end of the session approached, the contenders for pole position went back out on track, except for Michael Schumacher. Did the championship leader believe that the track conditions had deteriorated too much to hope for a faster lap? The facts proved him right. The sky had become overcast, lowering the track temperature, and no one was able to improve their times. The pole position, therefore, went to the German, who would have his compatriot Frentzen alongside him on the front row. Senna would share the second row with Ralf Schumacher. "Not bad for a recently retired driver!" Prost thought to himself as he went to join Senna in the garage to congratulate him.

Circuit de Nevers-Magny-Cours, Sunday, June 29, 1997

As he positions his race car on the starting grid, Ayrton Senna scans the horizon. The sun is shining just minutes before the start, but he spots dark clouds approaching the circuit. With nothing to lose, he suggests to Alain Prost to bet on the rain's arrival and adjust their settings accordingly. The former driver would have likely agreed immediately, but as the team boss he has become, he appears more hesitant. Aware that a great result is within his driver's reach, he fears that such a risky strategy might annihilate all hopes born from their excellent qualifying session. After consulting the increasingly pessimistic weather forecasts one last time, he finally gives his consent, hoping that the expected rain will arrive quickly.

Minutes before the start, Prost's mechanics are busy around car number 14. Its wings are adjusted a few notches to provide better traction on a wet track. The Brazilian knows he will lose time at the beginning of the Grand Prix, but with the rain coming, he could become the fastest man on the track and make his way to the front.

Hounded by television crews, he graciously answers their questions before equipping himself and isolating himself in his cockpit. Even though he is about to participate in his 162nd Grand Prix, it is his first Formula 1 start in over three years, and he needs to concentrate. He hasn't forgotten the reasons that led him to abruptly interrupt his career in 1994, but in that moment, surrounded by 21 other cars, he feels completely in his element. The competitive spirit has never left him.

At exactly 2 o'clock, the pack is released for the warm-up lap. Ayrton takes care to zigzag in order to bring his tires up to temperature. He takes advantage of this slow lap to recall the start procedure his engineers have taught him. Ahead of him, Michael Schumacher leads the way and sets the pace for the rest of the pack. Returning to the starting grid, the Prost comes to a halt in its designated spot just behind the Ferrari of the double German world champion. In his rearview mirrors, he keeps an eye on the rest of the grid while monitoring his temperatures. After a few seconds, he spots the green flag waved by the marshal responsible for signaling any incidents at the start. The five red lights illuminate one after the other. At that moment, the hearts of the 22 drivers race, and the engines, revved up to high RPM, roar through the Nivernais countryside. From the pole position, Schumacher makes a flawless getaway. Heinz-Harald Frentzen, positioned alongside him, shows more hesitation, which doesn't escape Senna. In just 150 meters, the Prost has passed the Williams and dives on the inside of the leader's Ferrari.

In the long Estoril corner, which determines the top speed until the Adelaide braking zone, Senna manages to maintain the advantage by taking advantage of the battle between Frentzen, Eddie Irvine, and Ralf Schumacher behind him. Schumacher approaches the hairpin with several lengths ahead of Senna, who already sees his opponents growing in his rearview mirrors. His "wet track" settings penalize his top speed. However, they give him a slight advantage in the twisty sections. At the end of the first lap, Schumacher already has a lead of more than one and a half seconds over Senna. The Paulista is ahead of Frentzen, Irvine, who had a brilliant start, and Villeneuve, who managed to get the better of Ralf Schumacher. For Senna, the most challenging part will now be to resist the attacks from the fast Williams-Renault, which is faster than him on the straightaways.

By the fifth lap, Schumacher had soared into the lead, setting a pace of over two seconds per lap. Behind him, Ayrton was finding it increasingly difficult to hold off the attacks from Frentzen, who in turn was being pursued by a pack consisting of Irvine, Villeneuve, and Ralf Schumacher.

In the slipstream of the Prost, at the end of the pit straight, Frentzen lost contact each time in the Estoril corner, which the Prost negotiated faster due to its aerodynamic grip. With a better top speed on the following straight, the Williams then closed in on Senna, but the Brazilian managed to stay ahead for now by braking very late and leaving him little room to pass.

On the seventh lap, a struggling blue car appeared on the giant screens. It was the second Prost driven by

Shinji Nakano, which had ended up stuck in the gravel after a spin. Alain Prost could now only rely on Senna to defend the team's interests. He had already given up hope for a possible honorable position for his second car. The Japanese, a mediocre driver imposed by Honda, had been stuck in the midfield of the standings. He had shown some progress by securing sixth place in Montreal, but Panis' accident had overshadowed that performance.

As their fuel loads decreased and their tires degraded, Senna and Frentzen were losing less time compared to Schumacher. However, the German remained glued to the rear wing of the Prost and did not ease the pressure.

Finally, taking advantage of a brief hesitation from Ayrton due to a yellow flag deployed to signal Jos Verstappen's off-track excursion, Frentzen made a move and broke free. This happened on the fifteenth lap.

On the command bridge, Alain Prost and Cesare Fiorio gaze at the sky, hoping to see large clouds that would bring rain. But for now, the sun still prevails. Are they losing their bet?

By the twentieth lap, the track is still dry, and Schumacher leads with a comfortable 25-second advantage over Frentzen, while Senna is nearly half a minute behind the leader with his "friend" Irvine close behind.

Two laps later, the leading Ferrari is the first to dive into the pit lane for a pit stop. In precisely eight seconds of being stationary, it emerges with four new tires and a full fuel tank. Spotting the Ferrari exiting the acceleration lane, Heinz-Harald Frentzen doesn't even take the opportunity to temporarily take the lead of the race.

On the next lap, Frentzen himself makes his pit stop, followed a few seconds later by the Ferrari of Eddie Irvine. This temporarily frees Ayrton from any pressure as Ralf Schumacher is over five seconds behind him.

At Prost's camp, there is a split opinion regarding whether to keep Senna on track to take advantage of a possible rain shower and save a pit stop, or to bring him in immediately to try and rejoin ahead of Irvine. Seeing the dark sky at the end of the pit lane and to stick with the established strategy, they ultimately decide not to call in Ayrton for now, especially since his lap times are improving despite his worn tires.

Drawing from the last remaining liters of his fuel tank, Senna is eventually forced to make a pit stop at the end of the lap 31. The rain is still far away, and the bet is currently lost. When he rejoins the track after a lightning-fast stop of 7.6 seconds, Irvine and Villeneuve have already passed him, and he inherits fifth place.

A dozen laps later, while Eddie Irvine begins the second series of pit stops, rain continues to desperately elude Ayrton. Still in fifth place, he drives in isolation about fifty seconds behind the leader. Irvine's pit stop temporarily moves him up a position. However, Frentzen, who has been running at a similar pace to Schumacher since he has a clear track, manages to stay ahead of the Prost after his pit stop at the end of the lap 47.

There are just over 22 laps remaining when Alain Prost points out to Cesare Fiorio that a few drops of rain are starting to fall on the circuit. At that moment, Schumacher leads ahead of Frentzen, Villeneuve, and Senna, but the latter two have only made one pit stop.

Both men make their pit stops simultaneously on the lap 52. The rain is too light to switch to wet tires, so they continue on slicks.

The pace of the frontrunners has noticeably slowed down. In conditions more favorable to his setup, Senna becomes the fastest man on track behind Schumacher. With a half-second per lap, he closes in on Villeneuve's Williams. By the lap 60, he has caught up, and it is precisely at this moment that the rain intensifies, particularly at the Lycee corner where several drivers, including Damon Hill, nearly spin out. Schumacher himself gets caught out in the Estoril corner. With all four wheels on the grass, he manages to rejoin the track unscathed and without losing the lead of the race.

Villeneuve, who is competing for the championship, doesn't take any unnecessary risks when the Prost car number 14 makes a move on the inside of the same corner. In any case, he can do little given the significant difference in speed between the two cars at that point. Ayrton easily overtakes him and takes fourth place with Eddie Irvine in his sights. He has ten laps remaining to close a gap of about ten seconds. Noticing that some drivers, including Johnny Herbert, are significantly faster than the leaders since they switched to intermediate tires, Alain Prost questions Ayrton over the radio. Knowing that a pit stop will cost him just under 20 seconds but that he can expect to be about five seconds faster per lap than with his slicks, the Brazilian doesn't hesitate for long and asks to make a stop at the end of the lap 61. As he rejoins the track, he trails Villeneuve by a 16-second margin and Irvine's Ferrari by 28 seconds. On the next passage over the timing line, Villeneuve is less than 10 seconds ahead of him. At this pace, he will catch up to the Canadian in less than two laps, and as expected, he easily overtakes him at the Adelaide hairpin on the lap 63. At Ferrari, both cars remain on track. It is understandable for Schumacher as he still holds a comfortable lead of 27 seconds over Frentzen, who is also on slicks. However, the decision to keep Irvine on track puzzles Prost. He rubs his hands together in satisfaction. By the end of the lap 64, his driver has closed the gap to about ten seconds behind the Irishman, who is now a loser regardless of the outcome. Either he makes a pit stop and gets passed by Senna, or he persists but will struggle to resist the Prost with his slick tires.

At the end of the lap 66, Irvine now catches a glimpse of Senna in his rearview mirrors. There are six laps remaining before the checkered flag. That may seem like an eternity when you're driving over 5 seconds off Senna's pace. Since their first intense encounter during the 1993 Japanese Grand Prix, Ayrton knows that the Northern Irishman is a tough competitor and will put up a fight. He attempts his first attack at the

Estoril corner. From the outside, he positions himself alongside the Ferrari, but it seems like Irvine ignores his presence and doesn't deviate from his racing line, even if it means pushing the Prost onto the grass. To avoid going off track, Ayrton is forced to lift off the throttle, losing speed on the straight. However, thanks to better traction, he manages to catch up quite easily with his opponent, who positioned himself on the inside at the entry to the hairpin. This time, the hunter takes no risks and brakes well on the outside, following the ideal racing line. Irvine, carried by his speed towards the outside of the track in the curve, helplessly watches as Senna overtakes him on the right during the acceleration phase. In just a few hundred meters, the Ferrari disappears from his rearview mirrors. Now, there are 5 laps remaining in the Grand Prix. Ahead of Senna, Heinz-Harald Frentzen, also on dry tires, still holds a significant lead of about fifteen seconds. Facing their control screens, Prost and Fiorio start dreaming of a second-place finish that seems within their driver's reach. He is immediately informed via radio that if he maintains his current pace, he will have one final lap to try and overtake the Williams-Renault.

Senna, significantly faster than the other drivers on grooved tires, seems to be in a league of his own. He surpasses Frentzen two laps before the finish, surpassing even the expectations of his new team manager. More prudent than Irvine, the German driver doesn't attempt to resist and prefers to secure third place. This time, Ayrton only has to drive at his own pace until the checkered flag. Schumacher is too far ahead to be caught. Second place in a modest car after over three years of inactivity is already quite an achievement! At least that's what Alain Prost thinks, pleased to secure his team's third podium finish in just eight Grands Prix.

As Senna crosses the finish line, he salutes the mechanics of his team gathered against the wall. Over the radio, he expresses his gratitude, saying, "Thanks, guys, we did a great job together this weekend! Thanks, Alain, for trusting a retiree!" he adds, winking at his new boss.

During his victory lap, the Brazilian driver wins the favor of the mostly Prost Grand Prix supporters in the audience. Applauding the fiercest adversary of Alain Prost would have seemed utterly incongruous to some of them a few years ago. But today, he is their hero.

Upon arriving in the parc fermé, Senna is joined by the day's winner, who extends his hand to congratulate him. The two champions have never been the best of friends, but Schumacher has always held the utmost respect for Senna. And, between us, he is not displeased that Senna has taken significant points away from his championship rivals.

Ayrton joins Alain Prost, who is waiting by the barriers with his mechanics, before joining the two Germans on the podium.

- It's a shame that the rain arrived so late, he whispers to the Frenchman while embracing him.

- You still have trouble settling for second place! Alain replies, delighted with the result.

- I felt really comfortable, and with a few more laps, I think I could have attacked Schumacher.

- You know, you have already done so much for the team, and no other driver could have done better today in a Prost car, Alain concludes, letting him go towards the podium. After the prize-giving ceremony and the post-race press conference, Ayrton rejoins his team in the Prost GP garage. Just like they used to do during their time at McLaren, he meets Alain to debrief the race. But before they start, he asks for a few moments to make a phone call to Olivier Panis.

Back in France, starting his recovery, Olivier is surprised to hear Senna's voice on the other end of the line.

- Hello Olivier, I suppose you were watching the television this afternoon.

- Of course, Ayrton, you had a perfect race with my car. I congratulate you. But I must admit that your phone call surprises me while making me extremely happy.

- It's true that we don't know each other well because I retired just as you were starting, but when I got into your car this weekend, I thought a lot about you. I put myself in your shoes, and I'm sure I would have liked my replacement to call and check on me, which is why I picked up the phone.

- Regarding my injuries, the surgeries went well, and I'm in good hands with Professor Saillant. He confirmed that I'll be able to race again, maybe even before the end of the season.

- I'm glad to hear that, and as I told Alain, I want to confirm that I will obviously give you your seat back as soon as you're able to get behind the wheel.

- Thank you, Ayrton, and I hope it happens soon because the car is performing well. It makes me even more frustrated to be bedridden.

- Be patient, you're still young, and you have great years ahead of you. Focus on your rehabilitation; that's your challenge in the coming weeks.

- You're right, but I'm boiling inside. Anyway, your podium will boost the team, and I have no doubt that with your experience, you will help the car progress. I'm counting on you!

- I'll do my best, but regardless, know that I had a lot of pleasure driving an F1 car again. There's nothing better in life!

- Maybe we'll have the opportunity to race against each other in the coming months!

- "Who knows?" replies an enigmatic Ayrton before bidding farewell to his interlocutor.

Hockenheim, Thursday, July 24, 1997

The Grands Prix are following one another, and they are not the same for Ayrton Senna since his return to competition. After a remarkable performance at Magny-Cours, he fell back into the pack at Silverstone, where he could only manage eighth place. At Hockenheim, where he has already won three times, he hopes to turn things around and return to the front. This German Grand Prix marks the return of Gerhard Berger to competition after missing three races due to sinus problems. Worse than his health issues, the soon-to-be 38-year-old Austrian had the pain of losing his father in a plane crash earlier this month. Feeling down, he finds some comfort in the presence of his friend Ayrton in the paddock. The two men hadn't seen each other for months.

- Well! Did the retirement home organize a trip to Germany? the always mischievous Benetton driver exclaims upon seeing Ayrton in front of his team's truck.

- Gerhard! Ayrton replies, his face beaming. It's great to see some old faces. There are so many people here that I don't know.

- On Sunday, you won't see my face much because I'll be far ahead of you!

- We'll see about that! Ayrton responds with a challenging tone before shifting to a more serious expression. By the way, how are you doing, Gerhard?

- The sinus issue is resolved, but for the rest, it will take time. The sudden loss of my father has been particularly brutal, and I'm struggling to bounce back emotionally.

- It's still fresh, indeed. Getting back behind the wheel will help you overcome the ordeal. You'll have less time to dwell on it.

- That's true, but this tragedy and the forced break made me reflect. I'm 38 years old, and my career is more behind me than ahead. I don't know if I want to keep traveling the world for much longer to go in circles on a circuit.

- I had the same questions in 1994 after the accidents of Ratzenberger and Wendlinger. I made the decision to stop, and then you see, I'm back, and I feel like I'm in the right place today. Formula 1 is my whole life, even though I know I'm reaching the age limit as well.

- What are your future plans? Are you looking for a contract for next year?

- After my podium finish in Magny-Cours, I received many phone calls, but I still need to think about it. I talked to Alain, and he agrees with me, even though he dreams of having a Senna-Panis duo for '98. However, you know that I've never hidden my desire to race for Ferrari someday.

- Racing for Ferrari seems unlikely since Jean Todt has built the team around Michael. I can't see you in a role as a second driver.

- If Todt wasn't so respectful of contracts, I could have come to Ferrari in '93. We were close to an agreement, but you and Alesi had already signed.

- You can't blame him for being fair to his drivers!

- No, it's to his credit, actually, but I had dreamed of finishing my career in red, and you're right, it's probably impossible now.

- In the meantime, focus on your weekend. Now that I'm back, you won't have an easy time! Berger concludes mischievously as he walks away toward the Benetton motorhome. Little did the Austrian know that his playful remark would ring true. On Saturday's qualifying, he snatched the pole position ahead of Fisichella, Hakkinen, Schumacher, and Frentzen. Ayrton, on the other hand, had to settle for the tenth fastest time, placing him between Villeneuve and Irvine on the grid.

Hockenheim, Sunday, July 27, 1997

As is often the case at this time of year, the
Hockenheim circuit is sweltering with heat as the 22
drivers qualified for the German Grand Prix line up
on the grid after their warm-up lap. From his pole
position, Gerhard Berger makes an excellent start,
with Giancarlo Fisichella's Jordan-Peugeot right
behind him. The Italian missed out on pole by a few
hundredths of a second and is determined to make up
for it during the race. Starting from the middle of the
grid, Senna managed to avoid obstacles, and by the
end of the first lap, he is already in seventh position.
He took advantage of the contact between Irvine and
Frentzen, which forced both drivers to retire in the
pits, as well as the poor start by Ralf Schumacher in
the second Jordan. On his favorite circuit where he
had brought Ferrari back to victory in 1994, Berger
shows his dominance right from the early laps. With
almost a one-second gap on each lap, he pulls away
from Fisichella, who seems capable of holding off the
championship-leading Ferrari.

After five laps, Berger is leading comfortably with a
4.8-second gap over Fisichella and 6 seconds over
Schumacher. Hakkinen is a bit further back and trying
to withstand the pressure from Jean Alesi in the
second Benetton. Villeneuve, who is fighting for the
championship, is not performing well this weekend.
Ayrton has been following him since the start and

knows he can go faster. Without hesitation, he takes advantage of the Williams' slipstream and overtakes it with a splendid braking maneuver at the Jim Clark chicane.

With a clear track ahead of him, the Prost driver can now set his own pace. In eight laps, he has opened up a gap of over three seconds on Villeneuve, while Alesi in fifth place is only two seconds ahead of his car's nose.

At the end of the sixteenth lap, Ayrton sees Alesi veer to the right to enter the pit lane. He is the first front-runner to make a pit stop. The Frenchman is followed by his teammate on the next lap, temporarily relinquishing the lead to Fisichella. When Berger rejoins the track, he is fourth, sandwiched between Mika Hakkinen and Ayrton Senna.

This weekend, he's so far ahead of the pack that he only needs a lap and a half to overtake the Finn and return to his normal pace.

By the twentieth lap, Ayrton takes fourth place as Hakkinen makes a pit stop. One lap later, it's Michael Schumacher's turn to refuel. The German was starting to struggle and gradually lose ground to Fisichella.

At this stage of the race, Fisichella is leading with a 9-second advantage over Berger and 14 seconds over Senna, but except for the Austrian, these drivers have not made their pit stops yet.

Both Fisichella and Senna choose the end of the 24th lap to make their stops. When they rejoin the track,

Berger has already passed by, but Fisichella manages to hold onto second place just ahead of the duo of Alesi and Schumacher, who are battling for the final spot on the podium. Senna, on the other hand, falls back to sixth position behind Hakkinen's McLaren. After a lap to bring the tires up to temperature, he has a particularly high-performance set of tires and decides to launch an attack on his former teammate. Coming within a car length of the gray car on the straight leading to the pit lane, he makes a daring move just before the fast turn number 1, where he knows he has better grip than the Finn. The maneuver is audacious and catches Hakkinen by surprise, as he expected Ayrton to attack at the next chicane.

With nineteen laps remaining, the Prost now has a clear track ahead but trails by more than sixteen seconds behind Schumacher's Ferrari, who is putting significant pressure on Jean Alesi. The Frenchman even cut a chicane by braking too late. However, on the thirtieth lap, he returns to the pit for a second stop.

The current standings are as follows: 1. Berger 2. Fisichella 3. Schumacher 4. Senna 5. Hakkinen.

Unbeatable on this Sunday, Berger sets an infernal pace in the race and extends his lead to around twenty seconds over Fisichella when he makes another stop at the end of the 34th lap. The second fastest man on the track is Senna, who gradually reduces his gap to Schumacher. The race then loses one of the two contenders for the world title when Villeneuve spins out and has to retire.

As Berger rejoins the track, he finds himself in Fisichella's slipstream. It takes him less than a lap to regain the lead of a Grand Prix that seems destined for him in a fair manner. Senna, in fourth position, is running in isolation. He moves up to third on the 39th lap when Fisichella suffers a puncture in the right rear tire. On his way to a second podium finish in three races for Prost, he knows that Schumacher is too far away to hope for a better result.

At Ferrari, there are concerns about Schumacher's tire wear after Fisichella's puncture. Jean Todt wants to play it safe by making a quick pit stop, but Senna could take advantage and pass him given the gap between the two champions. With his main championship rival out of the picture, Ferrari's team manager decides not to take any risks and calls his driver to the pit on the 40th lap as they cross the start-finish line.

After a 5.8-second pit stop, Schumacher returns to the battle, sandwiched between Senna, three seconds ahead of him, and Hakkinen, three lengths behind the Ferrari. With his fresh tires, the German gains nearly a second per lap on Senna. Two laps before the checkered flag, he is tucked in the gearbox of the Prost. He makes his first overtaking attempt at the first chicane, but Senna positions himself on the inside, forcing his opponent to brake off the racing line into the dust. It's a missed opportunity for now, but the championship leader is far from giving up. In the slipstream of the Prost as they enter the stadium section, Schumacher abruptly shifts to the right, forcing Senna to take the turn on the outside line. Determined not to surrender so easily, the Brazilian resists, and wheel-to-wheel, the two negotiate this fast corner to the applause of tens of thousands of spectators. With a better position for the next turn, Senna maintains his advantage as they enter the final lap of the race.

In the pits, Alain Prost doesn't miss the intensity of this battle to the chagrin of her fingernails. On his control monitor, he sees his driver still leading as they brake for the first chicane.

In the fight for the championship, Schumacher now seems hesitant to risk a collision, knowing that at worst, he will still gain four points on Villeneuve with this third place. Senna, who has found himself in this situation before, understands it well and is determined to put up a fierce fight because he has nothing to lose.

As they approach the Ostkurve, Senna catches sight of the Ferrari growing larger in his rearview mirrors. To prevent Schumacher from making a move, he positions himself on the inside of the track. Both drivers delay their braking as much as possible, but like Jean Alesi earlier in the race, the German loses grip and is forced to cut through the chicane. There's only half a lap left to go, and he has lost several lengths to the Prost in this mishap. This time, Schumacher decides to surrender and wisely secures his third place on the podium. This result allows him to extend his lead over Villeneuve in the overall standings to eight points, a good outcome in the championship.

Under the checkered flag, Senna expresses his joy by raising his fist as if he had won the race. This second place in a modest Prost, starting from tenth on the grid, is more than deserving. Especially since he fought hard for it against one of the best drivers on the grid.

As he climbs out of his parked car in the parc fermé, he falls into the arms of Gerhard Berger. The Austrian has delivered an outstanding performance this weekend and secures the tenth victory of his career.

- I didn't expect to find you here, Berger mischievously whispers in his ear as he removes his helmet.

- To be honest, me neither, but the car was fantastic this afternoon, and I was able to adopt a great pace to climb up the rankings. But what you achieved this weekend is remarkable, and I congratulate you. You were untouchable from start to finish.

- I did warn you that you would only see my rear wing! replied the Benetton driver, shaking hands with Schumacher, who had just joined them after playing taxi with Fisichella, the other unlucky hero of the race.

Still excited from his duel with the Brazilian, Schumacher approached Ayrton with a broad smile on his face. While he lost a position with that late pit stop, the battle gave him a lot of pleasure.

- You really wanted that second place! the Ferrari driver exclaimed, warmly shaking his hand.

- It seems like you did too, retorted Senna with a smirk before continuing, You know, I probably wouldn't have held on for another lap because my brakes were overheating.

- Mine too, but we fought fair and square, and the crowd recognized it. Listen to their enthusiasm, concluded Schumacher, pointing to the packed stands of the Hockenheim stadium.

On the podium, Ayrton positioned himself to the right of his friend Berger. This hadn't happened since the 1992 Portuguese Grand Prix when they were teammates at McLaren. During the national anthems, the Austrian couldn't hold back his tears, undoubtedly thinking of his recently departed father.

Senna felt his friend's emotion and tried to comfort him with a few pats on the back. The trophies were then presented to the three drivers, concluding this beautiful Sunday with a generous shower of champagne.

Spielberg, Sunday, September 21, 1997

After a ten-year absence from the calendar, the Austrian Spielberg circuit is making a grand return to Formula 1. A shortened version of the old Österreichring, it consists of three long straights and a twisty section that forces engineers to tune the cars with intricate compromises.

The only driver, along with Ayrton, who experienced the old circuit is Gerhard Berger. He took advantage of his home Grand Prix to announce his retirement from competition at the end of the 1997 season. However, the talk of the paddock revolves around Ayrton Senna's full-time comeback to the sport starting in 1998. The Brazilian has indeed signed a contract for a single season with an option for an additional year with the McLaren-Mercedes team. Ron Dennis used all his influence to convince him to join. Ayrton, eager to return to competition after his three-year hiatus, didn't have any other choice if he wanted a competitive race car. He did try knocking on Ferrari's door, but Jean Todt had built the team around Michael Schumacher and refused to hire a second top driver.

In the Woking team, it's Mika Hakkinen who pays the price for this resounding recruitment. His contract coming to an end after four seasons with the team, the Finn was once again offered the position of the team's third driver, just like in the 1993 season. Initially hesitant about this idea, he ultimately resigned himself to accepting it due to the lack of available good seats for 1998. However, he secured an exit strategy by demanding to reclaim his race seat in the event of Senna's retirement at the end of the upcoming season.

Although generally faster than Coulthard, especially in qualifying, Hakkinen still hasn't won his first Grand Prix. On the other hand, the Scotsman, Coulthard, ended McLaren's three-year without victory by winning in Melbourne at the beginning of the year, followed by another win in Monza. These two victories tilted the balance in his favor when it came to choosing Senna's teammate.

At Spielberg, Ayrton Senna is preparing to compete in his final race with Prost Grand Prix. After a speedy recovery, Olivier Panis has been declared fit to return to competition starting from the Luxembourg Grand Prix, which will take place in a week at the Nürburgring circuit. With everything he has brought to the team in his few appearances, Alain Prost did try to offer him a contract for '98, but he knew very well that at 38 years old, Ayrton didn't have time to wait. He needed an immediately competitive car to hope for more world titles.

After his Hockenheim feat, the driver from São Paulo finished the Hungarian Grand Prix in fifth position between Michael and Ralf Schumacher before fading away on the fast circuits at the end of the summer. Forced to retire due to an engine failure at Spa-Francorchamps, he finished the Italian Grand Prix in a lackluster ninth place.

From the first free practice sessions on Friday, everyone noticed that teams using Bridgestone tires seemed particularly comfortable on this track. On Saturday during qualifying, Ayrton created a sensation by securing none other than pole position ahead of Jacques Villeneuve and Mika Hakkinen. His time of 1'10"297 gave him the advantage over the Canadian by just seven thousandths of a second. On the third row, Barrichello and Magnussen, the Stewart drivers, confirmed the good form of the Japanese tires, while Damon Hill, also on Bridgestone, qualified in seventh position.

In the press conference, Ayrton took care to describe corner by corner his qualifying lap before stating that it is probably one of his most perfect achievements. Knowing the Brazilian driver's expertise in pure attacking driving, the journalists present in the room could only agree.

In the Prost Grand Prix garage, this performance created euphoria. No one, especially not the pragmatic Alain Prost, would have imagined seeing one of their cars secure a pole position this season. Let's not forget that the team has only been in existence for a few months. However, there is concern about the reliability of the Honda engines on this acceleration-heavy circuit.

On Sunday morning, Senna appears in the paddock,

invigorated by his pole position from the previous day and the announcement of his return to McLaren. Congratulated by everyone he encounters on the way to his garage, he takes the time to greet all the mechanics of the team, most of whom have never worked on a pole position car for a Grand Prix.

Already in front of the computers, Alain Prost welcomes him with a warm embrace. He knows that he is experiencing his last race as Ayrton's team boss and begins to feel a certain emotion. In just a few weeks, the Brazilian has raised the team's level of play and earned valuable points. The weak point of the JS45 remains the reliability of its Mugen-Honda engine, and he hopes that with the arrival of Peugeot next year, he will be able to overcome this handicap.

- How do you feel this morning, Ayrton? Alain Prost asks.

- I'm in great shape! This pole position has multiplied my motivation and strength.

- Let's hope you can confirm it in the race. It would be truly fantastic as a farewell gift.

- If I get a good start, I should be able to build a gap in the opening laps compared to the Williams and Hakkinen. Their Goodyear tires struggle to warm up on this track. The uncertainty lies in their performance over long stints.

- You're right, it will all come down to the start

of the stints. That's when you'll need to attack, and if the Stewarts can help you escape, even better.

- We'll see. I still need to work on the start procedure this morning.

- You know, Ayrton, whatever happens this afternoon, I want to thank you for what you've brought to the team in these few races. You saved our season by scoring those significant points. It will feel strange to see you in the garage next door next year.

- And I thank you for giving me this opportunity to come back. I've regained the fighting spirit of my best years in F1, and to be completely honest, it bothers me a little to have to leave you all tonight.

- Nakano has a solid contract with Mugen. I tried everything to allow you to finish the season with Panis, but the Japanese have a sense of honor and commitment. Yet, you know how revered you are at Honda!

- Oh well, it will give me longer vacations. I'll still try to be present for at least one Grand Prix to familiarize myself with Mercedes' working methods.

- Ron called me after the announcement of your contract. He was over the moon and would have never believed it could happen.

- Ever since my return was announced, he has been hounding me to 'come back home,' as he puts it. And he succeeded, the rascal! I just hope the team will continue its progress because I don't have much time left. I need a winning car right away.

- You might have one in front of you, Alain mischievously replies, pointing at the blue car around which several mechanics are busy.

Unfortunately for both men, the Brazilian's race comes to an end shortly after the halfway mark in a cloud of smoke from his failing Mugen-Honda engine. However, he had made a perfect start and was set for a commanding lead, with Jacques Villeneuve unable to match his pace. As he walks back to the pits, he is cheered by the crowd, to which he responds by throwing his gloves and balaclava. Upon his return to the garage, he is applauded by his mechanics and receives apologies from the Mugen engineers, who are almost ashamed for not providing him with an engine capable of finishing the Grand Prix. Almost more disappointed than him, Alain whispers comforting words while placing his hands on Ayrton's shoulders. This image will feature in most press articles covering the Austrian Grand Prix. Thus ends the beautiful story of the improbable Prost-Senna reunion, but the Brazilian's eyes are now set on 1998 and McLaren, the team of his greatest triumphs.

Jérez de la Frontera, Sunday, October 26, 1997

A few weeks after his last Grand Prix in Austria, Ayrton Senna reconnects with the atmosphere of the paddocks by attending the final round of the season in Jerez, Spain. In the McLaren pit, he takes advantage of this weekend to familiarize himself with his future team's new working methods while witnessing the decisive Grand Prix for the world title.

Before the start of the race, Jacques Villeneuve leads the provisional standings with exactly the same number of points as Michael Schumacher but with 7 victories compared to 5 for the German. The Ferrari driver took advantage of Villeneuve's disqualification at Suzuka for not respecting yellow flags to close in on him before the ultimate race.

The day before, during qualifying, the numerous spectators were treated to an exceptional spectacle with an unprecedented result. Indeed, Villeneuve took pole position with a time of 1'21.072, but Schumacher, in second place, and Frentzen, in third, recorded the exact same time to the thousandth of a second as the Canadian. As the regulations dictate in such cases, the grid order corresponds to the order in which the three drivers completed their best laps during the session. Ayrton, being a knowledgeable enthusiast, appreciated the true value of this extremely rare and exciting event, with the prospect of a thrilling duel between the two contenders for the ultimate crown.

With a better start than his rival, Schumacher immediately takes the lead ahead of Frentzen. Seeing the Ferrari pulling away, the Williams team orders the German to let Villeneuve pass on the eighth lap. After the first round of pit stops, Schumacher still leads, but Villeneuve has closed in on the Ferrari. In the McLaren pit, Ayrton is pleased with the team's good strategy, which has managed to place both their drivers ahead of Frentzen after the pit stops.

On the 45th and 47th laps, Schumacher and Villeneuve, respectively, make their final pit stops. Back on the track, the German seems to be experiencing difficulties, which does not go unnoticed by the Williams driver. Without hesitation, he launches an attack on the Ferrari at the end of the longest straight of the Andalusian circuit. After a late heavy braking, he positions himself to the right of the red car. Schumacher sees him alongside. He tries to cut across to the Williams, but he knows that in the event of a collision and double retirement, he will lose the title and leaves just enough space for Villeneuve to pass.

After three laps trailing just behind the Canadian, the Ferrari seems to have regained performance with tires finally reaching optimal temperature. The German must finish ahead of his rival to have any hope of winning the crown. Without hesitation, he positions himself right under the wing of the leader as they negotiate the fast Sito Pons corner. With a speed advantage thanks to the slipstream effect, he pulls out of Villeneuve's slipstream just before entering the heavy braking zone of Dry Sack. Stuck on the outside, the Quebecois driver leaves just enough space for Schumacher to pass, but he pushes his braking to the limit. The two cars enter the hairpin side by side. Upon acceleration, Schumacher widens his trajectory to force Villeneuve to give up, but the Williams driver keeps full throttle and puts two wheels on the grass. The next two corners are left-handers, which should favor him. Villeneuve on the left, Schumacher on the right, the two rivals negotiate them side by side, each hoping that the other will eventually yield, which doesn't happen. The upcoming Angel Nieto corner should settle the score. This time, it's Schumacher who has the advantage by driving on the right side of the track.

Determined to win this decisive duel, the German takes the Williams to the left to have a better trajectory when approaching the corner. Under braking, the Ferrari locks up its front wheels. Its driver couldn't delay the maneuver any further without running straight and taking the Williams with him. On the outside, Villeneuve brakes while straddling the curbs and suddenly loses grip. The struggling Williams car ends up in the gravel trap. With the desperation, Villeneuve slams on the accelerator pedal to get back on track. However, his flat bottom is stuck in the gravel, preventing him from getting back in the race, even though small movements of his car give him a glimmer of hope. By playing with his steering wheel, he finally manages to free himself from this trap, but the McLarens of Coulthard and Hakkinen have already passed. He knows that the game is lost fairly, but there are still about fifteen laps to go, and who knows what can still happen.

Alone in the lead, Schumacher continues his race, listening for any suspicious sound in his cockpit. Only a mechanical failure can prevent him from securing his third world title. He doesn't want to think about it, but the idea keeps crossing his mind. In the Ferrari pit, Jean Todt is just as stressed as his driver.

As the leader enters the final five laps of the race, his exhaust emits an unusual sound as he passes in front of the pits. Watching their screens, the engineers quickly understand what is happening. Schumi's engine is now running on only nine cylinders. He is immediately instructed to slow down to prevent the situation from worsening.

With three laps remaining, Hakkinen attacks and overtakes Coulthard on the straight in front of the pits. The Finn quickly closes in on Schumacher, who has significantly reduced his pace. In the ultimate lap, Schumacher obviously doesn't attempt to resist and lets Hakkinen pass in the chicane. As long as he finishes ahead of Villeneuve, the title is his. Hakkinen is on his way to his first Formula 1 victory. Coulthard takes second place, giving McLaren its first one-two finish since the 1991 Japanese Grand Prix. Schumacher, with smoke coming out of his engine, crosses the finish line with a two-second lead over

Villeneuve. One more lap and the title would have gone to the Canadian.

In the Ferrari pit, there is an explosion of joy. One of their drivers finally wins the championship after eighteen long years without a title.

Senna, captivated by this suspenseful finale, heads towards the parc fermé. He wants to congratulate Hakkinen on his first victory. After 95 unsuccessful Grand Prix races, the Helsinki native is torn between the joy of finally getting his name on the scorecard and the disappointment of having to give up his seat to Senna. Nevertheless, he appreciates the embrace from the Brazilian champion before heading to the podium.

Schumacher, third and the new world champion, slowly emerges from his cockpit, shaking his head. Overwhelmed by emotion, he sits on the nose of his Ferrari, removing his helmet and balaclava. In tears, he finally runs towards his mechanics, who are eagerly waiting behind the barriers. After shaking dozens of hands, his eyes meet Ayrton's, who is still standing next to the McLaren mechanics. Sportsmanlike, the Brazilian invites him to come closer to congratulate him in return with a firm handshake.

Now equals in terms of world championship titles, he takes the opportunity to arrange a meeting for the following year. The aborted duel in 1994 can now resume.

Melbourne, Albert Park, Sunday, March 8, 1998

Still soaked in sweat and champagne, Ayrton poses alongside David Coulthard and the members of the McLaren team for the commemorative photo of their one-two finish at the Australian Grand Prix.

For his return to Woking, the three-time world champion didn't hold back, securing pole position on Saturday with a time of 1'29"817 and clinching his 42nd victory after a perfectly controlled race. To top it off, he also set the fastest lap of the race. In Formula 1 jargon, that's called a hat trick.

Although Coulthard was quite close to his new teammate throughout the weekend, he was never able to challenge him for the win in this opening round of the 1998 season. The competition faced a harsh reality. The MP4/13 cars had a clear advantage in terms of performance. As evidence, Heinz-Harald Frentzen, third on the podium, finished the Grand Prix with a lap behind the Brazilian.

If the other teams don't step up their level, the championship could become a fratricidal duel between the McLaren pair, reminiscent of the legendary seasons of 1988 and 1989. Moreover, Coulthard seems to possess the qualities to give Senna a tough time. The Scotsman, praised by the entire paddock for his sportsmanship and behavior on and off the track, admires his teammate and doesn't forget that it was thanks to him that he was able to become an F1 driver in 1994. However, competition is competition, and he has no intention of settling for a role as a number two in this team.

Naturally, Ayrton leaves Australia leading the World Championship, a position he hasn't held since the 1993 Monaco Grand Prix. In three weeks, he will be welcomed as a hero in his hometown of Interlagos, where he hasn't raced in four years.

Interlagos, Saturday, March 28, 1998

A few minutes before the start of the qualifying session for the Brazilian Grand Prix, Ayrton puts on his racing suit at the back of the McLaren garage. His pensive expression reveals a certain annoyance. Hindered by multiple technical issues during the first two practice sessions, he has had very little track time the day before and had to rely on the morning session to fine-tune his setup. For this race, which he considers one of the most important of the season, he had dreamed of a better start to the weekend.

Frustrated to see their idol stuck in the garage, the thousands of Ayrton's fans who had filled the stands of the old Interlagos circuit since Friday had loudly expressed their disappointment. To compensate for their letdown, he didn't hesitate to come and meet them between practice sessions, carrying autographed caps. It almost led to a riot, but this communion with his fans had a boosting effect on his motivation.

The official FIA clock shows 2:00 PM. The serious business is about to begin for the twenty-two drivers entered in the Grand Prix. The first one to take to the track is Ricardo Rosset, a local driver as well. His modest Tyrrell car doesn't allow him to perform well, and his appearance on the track is only greeted by timid encouragement from the stands. The sea of gray-clad people is focused solely on Ayrton and makes it known with the sound of air horns as soon as their idol, still in the garage, appears on the giant screens.

The first significant lap time is set by Heinz-Harald Frentzen with a 1'18"109. It is at this moment that Senna chooses to make his first attempt. His exit from the pit lane is covered by the noise of the spectators screaming their support for the championship leader.

After a warm-up lap, he triggers the timing beam at full speed on the straight. A perfect braking allows him to negotiate the challenging Senna S curves with the best possible trajectory, named after him since his retirement from racing in 1994. With excellent balance, his McLaren exits the Curva do Sol at full throttle and speeds towards the rise of the lake. The almost right-angle turn that follows is devoured with a fierce flick of the steering wheel, while his first intermediate time is displayed on the screens. He already has nearly four-tenths of a second advantage over Frentzen.

In the stands, the crowd erupts and holds its breath until the second split, which Ayrton crosses, relegating the Williams driver to over six-tenths of a second behind. He only has to finish his lap calmly to comfortably take the top spot in the rankings. But in these moments, "calm" is not the word that immediately comes to mind for the Brazilian, who has decided to stun the competition and offer his fans the most beautiful of pole positions.

At the start of the final braking point of Junção, which determines the long uphill stretch towards the pits, he dives towards the inside and places his left wheels on the imposing painted kerb in the colors of his national flag. Perhaps he wanted to do too much because the challenge is truly demanding and unsettles the McLaren, which is catapulted towards the outside of the track. It takes more than that to impress its driver, who swiftly corrects the beginning of a spin with a precise flick of the steering wheel while keeping the throttle fully open.

Despite the time lost, he did not want to admit defeat to the turn that had cost him the race in 1994 and continues his effort until he crosses the finish line in 1'17"638. A few seconds later, David Coulthard, who did not make any mistakes, sets the second-fastest time in 1'17"757.

Back in the garage, Ayrton is congratulated by his mechanics, but he still wears a gloomy expression despite the pole position within his reach. He is disappointed with his driving mistake and is determined to go on the attack once again.

Around the circuit, the crowd is unaware of their idol's disappointment and begins to celebrate what looks like another pole position. This afternoon, only the McLarens seem capable of breaking the 1'18" barrier per lap, and Coulthard was unable to improve on his second attempt. But that doesn't matter, as three minutes before the checkered flag, the Mercedes V10 engine of the McLaren No. 8 roars in the British team's pit. Today, Ayrton has decided to humiliate his opponents and goes on the attack, determined to set an even faster time.

When he appears on the television screens, accelerating down the pit straight, he is following Johnny Herbert, who is completing his fast lap. Tucked right behind the Sauber's rear wing, he maximizes the drafting effect to gain a few km/h. Just before the braking point for the S-turns, the British driver moves to the left to let Ayrton pass. With the same mastery as his previous lap, he conquers the first sector, further improving his time. He knows that if he doesn't make any mistakes, he can go below 1'17" because he estimates that his slip-up cost him at least half a second.

As he approaches the famous left turn, he takes great care to avoid the inside kerb, brushing it with formidable precision. Finally, on the screens, Ayrton's time appears: 1'16"811! On equal footing, he puts nearly a full second on Coulthard.

In his car, he knows he has achieved a great performance, and his deceleration lap feels like a victory lap. He returns to the pit lane amid the cheers of his fans, sending them grand gestures of gratitude. After years of drought, he is delighted to experience this communion with his public once again, a connection he had missed so much.

Interlagos, Sunday, March 29, 1998

Between Ayrton Senna and his home Grand Prix, the history has never been simple. He had to wait until 1991 to finally win in Brazil, after seven unsuccessful attempts. Paradoxically, his rival Alain Prost achieved success on the Jacarepagua circuit in the 1980s before the race was moved to his hometown of Sao Paulo in 1990.

A second victory in 1993, driving a McLaren-Ford that was considerably less competitive than the Williams-Renault cars of Prost and Hill, further enhanced Senna's legendary status, thanks to his skills in wet conditions.

As was often the case in the past, Ayrton had the most competitive car on the grid this Sunday. However, he knew, especially in Brazil, that victory was far from assured despite his dominant performance in qualifying.

Nevertheless, in a perfect scenario, the McLaren driver had an ideal first half of the race. Taking the lead at the start and exerting total control over the race while gradually distancing himself from Coulthard, the only driver capable of challenging him, Ayrton was on his way to a third victory at Interlagos, much to the delight of the enthusiastic home crowd. Seasoned Formula 1 fans might lament the complete absence of suspense, but such considerations were far from the minds of the Brazilian champion's fans, who were thrilled to see their idol return to his home race after three years of retirement.

It must be said that Interlagos had rarely witnessed such excitement. The overcrowded grandstands were adorned with the yellow and green colors of the Brazilian flag, as thousands of flags were frantically waved by spectators who had eyes only for the McLaren No. 8. Law enforcement had to request reinforcements to control the hundreds of gatecrashers attempting to access the circuit without tickets. Seats were sold out within hours of the announcement of the Brazilian's contract signing with McLaren.

We are on the 64th lap of the race, and Senna has once again improved the lap record. His lead over his teammate is around fifteen seconds. Michael Schumacher, in third place, is nearly a minute behind. The McLarens are truly in a league of their own this weekend. There are still eight laps to go before the checkered flag is waved. Ayrton has experienced this situation dozens of times in his career, but here, at his home race, it feels a bit different. He doesn't want to miss out on this victory, which is why he becomes increasingly cautious as the finish line approaches.

He takes care not to cut the corners too closely to minimize the risk of a puncture, ensures that the driver ahead of him sees him when he laps a backmarker, and listens attentively for any suspicious sounds in his cockpit. But there's nothing to report on that front either. His MP4-13 has shown no defects since the beginning of the Grand Prix. Only the intermittent gusts of wind blowing across the Interlagos neighborhood have occasionally disrupted his progress.

At the start of the 65th lap, his race engineer is alerted by the sight of an object obstructing one of the side air intakes of his car. Upon reviewing the replay, he realizes that it's the fabric of a flag that has been blown by the wind from one of the grandstands. After a few hundred meters with this intruder, he notices that the engine temperature of the car is dangerously rising, which he immediately reports to his driver via radio.

- Ayrton, there's a flag stuck in an air intake on the right side of the car. The engine temperature is becoming critical.

- Yes, I can see that, but what can I do?

- You have a bit of margin. Try to slow down to stay within an acceptable range.

- Okay, I'll reduce the maximum revs. How many laps are left?

- Seven laps, Ayrton, and David is sixteen seconds behind you.

After this brief exchange, the Brazilian driver complies and reduces his pace by nearly two seconds per lap. Unfortunately, it doesn't have the desired effect, and the temperatures continue to dangerously flirt with the red zone.

- Ayrton, it's still not working. You have to slow down even more, otherwise, you won't be able to finish the race.

- If I slow down any further, I can kiss the victory goodbye, Senna responds irritably.

- Try shaking the car to see if you can dislodge it, his engineer advises in desperation.

In the grandstands, there's confusion and concern. The spectators observe their champion's lead melting away rapidly, and they see the McLaren swerving violently on the straights. Usually, drivers do that during the warm-up lap to heat up their tires, but at the end of the race, it doesn't make sense. Ayrton must be facing a problem.

- There's nothing more I can do. That damn flag is stuck for good! Senna announces after several futile attempts.

- I only see one solution, Ayrton. You need to come to the pit lane so we can remove it, and you need to do it quickly because your engine won't hold up much longer.

With six laps remaining, Ayrton calculates his options. A pit stop without refueling should cost him just under twenty seconds. With a fifteen-second advantage over Coulthard, he is guaranteed to rejoin the track behind the Scotsman. Closing a four to five-second gap in six laps, with equal tire wear and conditions, seems nearly impossible, not to mention attempting an overtaking maneuver. In a flash, he makes his decision and announces it over the radio.

- Alright, I'll stop at the next opportunity, but prepare a set of fresh tires for me.

- Ayrton, just to confirm, you want to change tires during your pit stop? the engineer asks, beginning to grasp the gamble his driver is about to take.

- Yes, I confirm it.

As the spectators see the gray McLaren entering the pit lane, a tremendous roar of disappointment fills the air. Their idol will not win this afternoon.

Each in their position, the mechanics are focused on their task. The car comes to a perfect stop in its designated spot. In a well-rehearsed ballet, the four tires are replaced while the flag is swiftly removed by a team member. As the car continues to roll at a reduced speed towards the pit lane exit, Coulthard's second McLaren crosses the finish line and takes the lead.

By choosing to replace his tires, Ayrton lost nearly four additional seconds. However, he hopes to make up for this delay with better grip. Starting the final five laps, he trails his teammate by seven seconds, but now his engine is running smoothly, and his new tires are at their optimal temperature. As for his motivation to secure this victory, it is heightened by this twist of fate. Under these conditions, the three-time world champion is irresistible, as Coulthard realizes at the start of the penultimate lap when he sees Senna closing in on him. With a gain of two seconds per lap, Senna now has less than two laps to try and snatch the victory from his teammate.

In front of his screens, Ron Dennis begins to feel the stress creeping in. Even though he has complete confidence in his two drivers, he can't help but think of the catastrophe that would ensue if the two team cars collided. Especially since a second consecutive one-two finish is within reach. At McLaren, team orders are rejected, and both drivers are free to compete as long as it doesn't harm the team.

In this penultimate lap, Ayrton doesn't attempt any overtakes. He wisely studies his opponent's weaknesses by staying glued to his rear wing. He makes his first overtaking attempt at the end of the pit straight. Knowing that it's the best spot on the circuit to pass, Coulthard has anticipated this maneuver and firmly defends his position by braking to the left side of the track. Despite a late braking move, Ayrton falls slightly short of executing an outside overtake in the following esses.

Fueled by the crowd's support, which he can hear cheering despite the roar of his V10 engine, he refuses to give up until the checkered flag is waved at him.

In the twisty section of the track, he takes advantage of his superior grip to hound the Scot, but Coulthard maintains his composure and sportsmanship by blocking his advances. Just a few meters from the finish line, Ayrton knows that he only has the long straight leading to the pits for one final attack. Intentionally, he allows himself to slightly drop back in Mergulho to negotiate the Juncao corner at full speed without being disturbed by the aerodynamic wake of the leading car. This twelfth turn of the track determines the straight where he plans to make his move.

Thanks to his fresher tires, he exits the corner with a slight speed advantage over his teammate. Meter by meter, he closes in on his prey, feeling the effects of the drafting phenomenon. Just before the final Arquibancadas corner, he pulls out to the left. Now, both men can do nothing to change the outcome of this race, except keep their foot on the accelerator until the end of the straight.

Silver arrows cross the finish line side by side. From the stands, the spectators are unable to see who crossed the timing line first. In a collective reflex, all heads turn towards the giant screen. Only technology can determine the outcome. After a few seconds of suspense, during which even the two drivers find themselves in anticipation, the verdict is announced. Ayrton Senna is declared the winner with a 0.008-second advantage over Coulthard. At 300 km/h, that's barely 66 centimeters! Even before his victory is confirmed through the radio, Ayrton realizes that he has added a third Brazilian Grand Prix win to his record as he sees the crowd rise as one and express their joy loudly.

With such a tiny margin, the record set at Monza in 1971 is surpassed by just two thousandths of a second. While thanking his fans, he remembers a similar ending to the race in Jerez in 1986, when he battled Nigel Mansell. The difference was that back then, Mansell played the role of the hunter after a late tire change. Although the gap at the finish line was only 0.014 seconds, Mansell managed to withstand the attacks from the Williams.

Back in the pit lane after a memorable victory lap, Ayrton brings his machine to a stop at the foot of the podium. Overwhelmed by emotion, he timidly expresses his joy by raising his arms in front of the camera, capturing every moment. Sitting on the sidepod of the McLaren, he takes the time to remove his helmet and gloves. With teary eyes, he slowly approaches his mechanics gathered behind the barriers. One by one, he thanks them for the work they've done over the weekend before heading to participate in the podium ceremony.

During the press conference, he dedicates this victory to Flavio, his brother-in-law who passed away two years earlier in the same city where he has just achieved one of his greatest successes in Formula 1. His sister Viviane, watching the televised broadcast from the McLaren hospitality area with her children, cannot hold back her tears. She truly did not expect such a heartfelt tribute.

Imola, Thursday, April 23, 1998

Having arrived the previous evening in the Imola region to participate in the San Marino Grand Prix, Ayrton arrived very early at the gates of the Enzo and Dino Ferrari circuit. He felt no apprehension about driving again on this track despite his terrible accident in 1994. It must be said that the frightening Tamburello corner had just been cut by a chicane to slow down the cars.

It took a new miracle for a decision to finally be made regarding this dangerous turn. It happened the previous year during the qualifying session. Behind the wheel of his Minardi-Hart, Ukyo Katayama broke his suspension while pushing to the limit through the first sector of the circuit. This break sent him crashing at over 250 km/h into the infamous wall that had already caused many scares for Piquet, Berger, and Senna. Dazed by the impact but unharmed, the Japanese driver escaped with a simple concussion. For the fourth time, the worst had been avoided, leading the governing bodies of Formula 1 to demand a modification of this corner. Relying on luck had been enough.

As he often does when arriving at a circuit, Ayrton takes advantage of the calm morning to ride his bicycle along the track. He discovers the new chicane and already starts imagining the ideal trajectory to negotiate the corner at its best. Without a glance towards the site of his 1994 accident, he then heads towards the Tosa corner. However, about a hundred meters before reaching the hairpin, he veers left onto the grass and gets off his bike, leaning it against the wall. It is at this spot that four years earlier Roland Ratzenberger lost his life, colliding head-on with the concrete wall.

In the solitude of this spring morning, Ayrton takes a moment to reflect, perhaps reciting a prayer for the departed Austrian driver. This is what two marshals, setting up their equipment in preparation for the Grand Prix near the Brazilian, assume. Sensing that the timing is probably not appropriate, they decide not to approach him for an autograph and watch him pedal away on his mountain bike.

Monaco, Monday, May 25, 1998

The clock in his Monaco apartment is nearing noon as Ayrton slowly emerges from his sleep. He had spent the previous night celebrating his seventh victory in the Principality, surrounded by members of his team and close friends. A lingering migraine reminds him that champagne had flowed freely, and it's time for him to head to the shower to help his metabolism get back on track.

With this fourth win of the season, following Melbourne, Sao Paulo, and Barcelona, he leads the World Championship with a comfortable 17-point advantage over his teammate Coulthard. Schumacher, who won the Argentine Grand Prix ahead of him, is in third place, five points behind the Scotsman. If it weren't for a gearbox failure that caused his retirement in Imola, he could have achieved even better results, but mechanical failures are part of Formula 1. Besides, his main rivals have also faced their fair share of troubles.

As the hot water splashes on his face, he can't help but reflect on that fateful Monaco Grand Prix in 1994, during which he abruptly put a (temporary) end to his F1 career. What a stark contrast between that day when he had contemplated giving up everything and this post-celebration morning after securing his 45th victory on his beloved circuit.

Refreshed by his shower, Ayrton puts on casual attire and steps out of his apartment to grab a bite to eat at his favorite restaurant. As he strolls through the streets of the Principality, his attention is drawn to a familiar figure. Walking towards him, he recognizes Erik Comas, the former French Formula 1 driver who raced for Ligier and Larrousse between 1991 and 1994. Comas was a great prospect in the sport after winning the International Formula 3000 Championship in 1990 but was unable to fulfill his potential in F1 due to a lack of competitive machinery. Shaken, much like Ayrton, by the tragedies of the 1994 season, he decided to redirect his career to Japan, becoming a Nissan driver in the local Grand Touring championship. Currently leading the overall standings in the 1998 season, he was in Europe for a promotional event organized by a sponsor.

Although they hadn't seen each other for four years, a special bond connects Ayrton to Erik since the 1992 Belgian Grand Prix. During Friday's free practice session, Comas lost control of his Ligier in the Blanchimont corner, a flat-out sweeping turn. The blue car came to rest in the middle of the track after violently hitting the barrier. Inside the cockpit, the driver from south of France lost consciousness. In the impact, a wheel struck his helmet, rendering him unconscious. What was even more concerning was that his foot was still pressing the accelerator while fuel was leaking from the side of the Ligier. If, by unfortunate circumstances, the highly flammable liquid had reached the burning engine, Erik Comas would have been trapped in flames.

A few seconds after the accident, the first car to arrive at the scene was Senna's red and white McLaren. Realizing the gravity of the situation and driven by his courage, the Brazilian parked his car a few dozen meters away from the wreckage, unfastened his harness, and ran towards it, weaving through the cars arriving at full speed. Upon hearing the roaring Renault V10 engine, Ayrton hurried to activate the cut-off switch, eliminating any risk of fire. Following this incident, Comas believed that Ayrton, with his swift reaction, had quite simply saved his life.

- Well, Erik, what a surprise! Ayrton exclaimed.

- Ayrton! It's great to see you! And congratulations on your impressive victory yesterday! replied Comas.

- Thank you very much. It was an emotional moment, four years after my first retirement here under the conditions you know, Ayrton acknowledged.

- Especially considering that you're the first driver to win the same Grand Prix seven times. A record that will be hard to beat, complimented Comas.

- I see you're well aware of my career! Ayrton chuckled.

- Even though I left F1 over three years ago, I'm still a passionate fan, Comas admitted.

- Have you had lunch, Erik? Ayrton asked.

- Not yet, I was about to head to Nice airport, but my flight is still three hours away, replied Comas.

- Well, in that case, you have no excuse. Follow me, you're my guest, Ayrton said, tugging at Comas' sleeve.

Seated at a discreet table arranged by the maître d'hôtel, the two drivers began their meal, reminiscing about the good old times. The conversation then drifted towards the current season when Erik Comas inquired about Ayrton's plans beyond 1998.

- I've signed with McLaren for just one season with an option for 1999, Ayrton responded.

- And do you think you'll exercise that option? Comas timidly asked, not daring to imagine that Senna would confide in him.

To his great surprise, and perhaps to Ayrton's surprise himself, the Brazilian took a deep breath before answering:

- To be completely honest with you, I think I'll retire at the end of the season if I win the championship. After reflecting on it and discussing with Alain, who did the same in

1993, I realized that my comeback was mostly motivated by the frustration of leaving F1 through the back door. By stopping with a fourth title, I would leave with peace of mind and then join Alain right behind the Great Fangio! he added with a mischievous smile.

Taken aback by this show of trust from the McLaren driver, despite not being particularly close, Erik Comas asked him:

- And does McLaren know about your decision?

- You're the first person I'm telling! Ayrton retorted with a hearty laugh, seeing the bewildered expression on the former Ligier driver's face after this revelation.

- I hope Ron Dennis finds out soon because it's quite a heavy secret for me to keep all by myself!

- The second person to learn about it will be Mika, as the future of his career depends on this decision. He accepted without a fuss the fact that he had to give up his seat for me, and I owe him that much. He is a talented driver who deserves much more than being a reserve driver. His first victory last year, after such a long wait, has probably relieved him of a burden, and I predict a brilliant future for him if McLaren remains as competitive next year.

- And when do you plan to tell him? Comas asked.

- Very soon, that way I'll have one more ally in my quest for the championship! Ayrton replied.

- I'm surprised by your praise for Mika. If I remember correctly, your relationship was particularly stormy when you were teammates in late '93.

- With hindsight, I have made my mea culpa. I was clearly dominating Andretti since the beginning of the season, and then he takes his place at Estoril and beats me right away in qualifying. I was furious, and I behaved poorly towards him, which had detrimental consequences on our relationship. In a way, being kept away from the circuits for three years allowed me to reflect on myself, and I came back this year with a different mindset.

Upon landing in Tokyo a few hours after this unexpected encounter, Erik Comas was still surprised by the confessions Ayrton had made to him. During that lunch, he had exchanged more with him than during the two or three seasons they had spent together on the circuits.

Circuit de Nevers-Magny-Cours, Sunday, June 28, 1998

Two hours after the arrival of the French Grand Prix, Ayrton is still fuming. Sitting in the McLaren motorhome, he keeps replaying the images of the race start. It happened in two stages because Verstappen, who was recently signed by Tyrrell to replace the disappointing Magnussen, stalled during the first start, which led to a restart being organized.

If things had stayed that way, Ayrton would have had a clear lead. However, at the second start, Michael Schumacher got a better launch than him, taking his teammate Irvine along. As they approached the Estoril turn side by side with the McLaren, the Northern Irishman was determined not to yield to the Brazilian, who had his eyes solely on his German rival's Ferrari. Positioned on the inside, Irvine had the advantage to exit the corner ahead of Senna, which he indeed did. But at the end of the following straight, there was the Adelaide hairpin, one of the main overtaking zones on the Burgundy circuit. Not wanting to let Schumacher get away, Senna stuck his nose into the gearbox of the Ferrari number 4, which immediately veered to the right side of the track to defend its second position. Undeterred, Ayrton had decided to go for it and took his chance on the outside, trying to make the most of his higher speed.

Braking as late as possible, both men heavily locked their wheels as they approached the turn. Being too close to each other and lacking full control of their cars, a collision was inevitable. Just like in 1992 after a contact with Schumacher's Benetton, Ayrton ended his French Grand Prix in the same hairpin. Irvine's Ferrari had suffered less from the crash, and the Newtownards native was able to finish the race in second place behind his teammate. For Ferrari, it was a complete triumph, marking their first one-two finish since the 1990 Spanish Grand Prix, eight years earlier.

Objectively, neither of the two drivers was to blame for the incident. They both had their share of responsibility. It was a 50-50 situation, a mere racing incident. However, considering the animosity between them since the 1993 Japanese Grand Prix and his pride, the McLaren driver believed that Irvine was entirely responsible for his retirement.

Ultimately, what bothers Ayrton on this Sunday evening is realizing that Michael Schumacher has closed the gap to just two points behind him in the overall standings after securing a second consecutive victory, despite not finishing the last two Grand Prix races due to a gearbox failure in Montreal.

After a superb start to the season, where he had built a comfortable lead in the championship, the points are now almost reset. This worries him even more, considering the evident progress of the Ferrari.

Silverstone, Sunday, July 12, 1998

Two weeks after his disappointment in Magny-Cours, Ayrton is determined to redeem himself at Silverstone. Having secured an undisputed pole position the day before, ahead of Michael Schumacher, he scans the sky as he positions his McLaren on the starting grid. The morning warm-up took place in heavy rain, but in the early afternoon, the precipitation is much lighter. Nevertheless, the track remains partially wet, and an intermediate tire start is necessary, especially as the sky continues to threaten.

As the lights go out, the leading McLaren cleanly pulls away from its spot with Schumacher's Ferrari in its wake. Qualifying in eighth place, Jean Alesi has leaped from his line to find himself in fourth position behind David Coulthard.

In the first few hundred meters of the race, Schumacher tries to keep up with Senna, but the Brazilian's pace in these conditions is phenomenal. To make matters worse, he loses his second place to the Scotsman at Abbey in the fourth lap.

After ten laps of racing, Senna is still in the lead with a seven-second advantage over Coulthard and ten seconds over Schumacher, but the rain is intensifying. The first victim of the track conditions, Damon Hill, loses control of his Jordan at Brooklands and retires on the fourteenth lap. Two laps later, it is Frentzen's turn to give up after a spin-out.

During the first round of pit stops, some drivers choose to stay on intermediate tires while others take the gamble of switching to full wet tires, like Schumacher on the nineteenth lap. McLaren doesn't put all their eggs in one basket. Coulthard, who stops at the end of the twenty-first lap, goes back out on intermediates, while Senna follows Schumacher's strategy two laps later.

Still in the lead, the Brazilian is gradually being caught up by his teammate because the track is not wet enough to fully exploit his tires. In just four laps, Coulthard is less than a second behind him. However, Schumacher, who is struggling like them with his wet tires, keeps a good distance from the McLarens.

The rest of the events will prove both championship contenders right. The rain intensifies, and several drivers fall victim to it, including Herbert, Salo, Rosset, and Tuero. In these conditions, Ayrton increases the gap between himself and Coulthard, who has no choice but to slow down to avoid ending his race in the gravel trap. But despite his cautious driving, Senna's teammate finds himself in a tricky situation at Abbey on the thirty-eighth lap. Wanting to lap Tora Takagi, he spins out and has to retire.

At that moment, Senna leads ahead of the two Ferraris of Schumacher and Irvine. After a second pit stop, the three men resume in that order.

As they enter the forty-first lap, torrents of rain now pour down on the English circuit. The number of spins and off-track excursions becomes countless, but Senna, still imperial in the deluge, continues to increase his lead over Schumacher, who is the only one capable of approaching the Paulista's lap times.

At the forty-fifth lap, Senna has a massive lead of fifty seconds over Schumacher, but the entry of the safety car onto the track will nullify all his efforts. Deemed impassable by the race officials, there are now only eleven remaining competitors on the track.

After five laps at reduced speed, the race is restarted, and the rain has completely stopped. Between the McLaren and the Ferrari is the Benetton of Fisichella, who is one lap behind. Eager to challenge Senna, Schumacher overtakes the Italian before the timing line, which is forbidden by the regulations.

This time, the situation has changed, and Senna is no longer as comfortable as before the neutralization. His tires have cooled down and lost a lot of grip, unlike Schumacher, who is now flying over the track. Despite all his attempts to resist, Senna has to surrender on the fifty-second lap. The German is on cloud nine and escapes in the lead. The Brazilian fumes under his helmet, unable to match the pace of his opponent. In just seven laps, he loses over thirteen seconds to the Ferrari.

But as the race enters its penultimate lap, the information appears on the control screens. Michael Schumacher is penalized with a ten-second stop-and-go penalty for his illegal overtake on Fisichella.

In the McLaren pit, they announce the information to Senna, who will now retake the lead of the race with just one lap remaining. However, as he passes by the pit lane, another sign is shown to him with the label "P2." Thinking it must be a mistake, Ayrton stays focused to avoid making a mistake so close to the finish.

One final pass through the Luffield corner, and Senna only needs to accelerate at Woodcote to cross the finish line as the winner of the ninth Grand Prix of the season. As he passes under the checkered flag, he raises a triumphant fist. He is back on the path to victory after two major disappointments.

But as he greets the crowd during his victory lap, his engineer informs him that he is actually in second place behind Schumacher. The German entered the pit lane, stopped at his designated spot for ten seconds, and returned to the track after crossing the finish line.

By serving his penalty in this manner on the final lap, Schumacher crossed the line before his opponent. Precisely 1.324 seconds ahead of Senna. He is declared the winner ahead of Senna.

In the parc fermé, the Brazilian engages in a heated discussion with his rival. According to him, Schumacher should have served his penalty at the end of the fifty-ninth lap since the penalty was communicated to him earlier. If he had done so, he would not have been able to retain the lead of the race. Ross Brawn, coming to the defense of his driver, tries to explain to Ayrton that the penalty was announced to them too late, and they had no other option but to proceed as they did.

Furious, Senna doesn't believe a word of it and vigorously expresses his thoughts to his two interlocutors, all under the watchful eye of the cameras. In the stands, spectators grow impatient, eagerly awaiting the trophy ceremony. An FIA official tries to reason with the McLaren driver, inviting him to appear on the podium, but Senna refuses and walks briskly back to his pit. Ultimately, only Schumacher, visibly disturbed by Senna's reaction, and his teammate Irvine will stand on the podium for a rather somber ceremony where even the champagne won't flow.

The McLaren team lodges a protest but doesn't succeed in their cause. Schumacher leaves Silverstone with a third consecutive victory and takes the lead in the championship by two points. As for Senna, he will face a hefty fine for not adhering to the protocol. Later in the evening, the Brazilian national football team will suffer a 3-0 defeat to France in the World Cup final. It certainly wasn't his day.

Spa-Francorchamps, Sunday, August 30, 1998

Sitting in the wet grass, Ayrton Senna is still shaken by the massive crash he just experienced. Undoubtedly one of the most terrifying of his career. He had just started the tenth lap of the race. Under heavy rain, the track conditions were appalling. That's when his McLaren began to hydroplane at the worst spot on the circuit, in the middle of the Eau Rouge uphill section, which is normally taken flat out in dry conditions. Propelled like a missile into the barriers, the silver car disintegrated before soaring and ending up on the other side of the fence, on the service road. Miraculously, no marshal or photographer was in the path of the uncontrollable projectile.

Unscathed, Senna emerged from the still-smoking wreckage of his survival cell, which had performed its role perfectly. Removing his helmet and then his balaclava, he appeared pale as a sheet in front of the television cameras. He did raise his thumb to signal to his loved ones that he was okay, but his face betrayed the fear he had just experienced. For the second time after Imola 1994, fate had done him a favor.

From the very start, the race had already taken on the aspect of a massacre. Losing control upon acceleration after La Source hairpin, David Coulthard caused the biggest pile-up in Formula 1 history. Thirteen cars were eliminated. After an interruption of the race, a second start was given, and most of the drivers involved in the accident were able to take the wheel of their spare cars.

Starting from pole position, Senna made a perfect start and managed to fend off Damon Hill's attacks in his Jordan-Honda. With better visibility than his competitors, he had built up a comfortable lead of nearly fifteen seconds before the crash occurred.

Escorted to his pit by a marshal, he finds himself on the team's command bridge while the safety car leads the race. Helpless to change the course of events, he can only witness Michael Schumacher's leading the race, having overtaken Damon Hill. He feels remorseful because if things remain as they are, the Ferrari driver will leave Spa as the championship leader.

Having achieved two impressive victories in Austria and Hockenheim, he had fallen victim to Schumacher's dominance in Budapest, with the German securing his win through a daring strategy orchestrated by Ross Brawn. At the same time, despite suffering from suspension issues, he managed to salvage a single point in the Hungarian Grand Prix. Despite this setback, he arrived in Belgium still holding a three-point lead in the overall standings.

In the McLaren garage, a gloomy atmosphere prevails. Their team leader has been eliminated after just 10 laps, while Coulthard finds himself at the back of the pack following a collision with a Benetton in the opening lap. On the other hand, for Ferrari's 600th Grand Prix, Schumacher is on cloud nine, consistently gaining three to four seconds per lap on Hill. However, the outcome is far from certain as the rain continues to fall relentlessly, and the risk of a spin-off looms at every moment.

We find ourselves at the 26th lap when Michael Schumacher is on the verge of lapping Coulthard, subjecting him to the humiliation of being overtaken. Following closely behind the McLaren at Blanchimont, the Ferrari is poised to make a move under braking at the Bus Stop chicane. Coulthard, aware of Schumacher's presence behind him, brakes earlier to facilitate the overtake. However, due to the water spray, Schumi fails to realize that the driver ahead has slowed down and crashes into him forcefully from the rear, ripping off his right front wheel.

Watching the scene unfold on the screen, Senna can hardly believe it. Schumacher has missed a golden opportunity to widen the gap in the championship. Driven by adrenaline and undoubtedly disappointment, the Ferrari driver angrily exits his car, which he managed to bring back to the pits. Swiftly removing his helmet, he rushes towards Coulthard's pit to express his strong disapproval. Ferrari team members try to dissuade him, holding onto his shoulder, but he pushes them aside before being finally blocked by a McLaren mechanic who denies him access to the pit. The exchange with Coulthard, who is still wearing his helmet, is brief, but from the bridge, Ayrton clearly hears his rival accusing his teammate of trying to kill him.

Knowing that he witnessed everything on the television screens, Senna understands that it is not the case and, on the contrary, David tried to make things easier for him by slowing down. Unfortunately, circumstances led to a bad outcome. That's racing... As proof, one lap later, Giancarlo Fisichella makes the same mistake at the same spot while lapping Shinji Nakano.

Only six drivers will cross the finish line of this epic Belgian Grand Prix. For the first time in their history, the Jordan team celebrates a victory in F1, and even a one-two finish as Ralf Schumacher secures the second position behind Hill and ahead of Jean Alesi.

With this success of the underdogs, who do not pose a threat to the championship, Senna leaves Spa with the feeling that he has done more than just limit the damage despite his driving error, and that is what matters most to him.

Suzuka, Sunday, November 1st, 1998

As Ayrton Senna turns off his alarm clock on Sunday morning, he struggles to get out of bed. He had great difficulty falling asleep the night before and would love to stay a little longer under the covers. For the fifth time in his life, he will compete for the Formula 1 World Championship title at the Suzuka circuit, in a country where he is often regarded as a living god. The statistics are clearly in his favor, as he only missed out on the 1989 title.

Once again, he is considered the favorite, as he holds a three-point lead over Michael Schumacher. After finishing second at Monza, he had once again lost the lead in the overall standings before setting things right by winning the Luxembourg Grand Prix ahead of the Ferrari driver.

During qualifying, he secured his thirteenth pole position of the season by a narrow margin ahead of the German. A significant gap separates the two title contenders from the rest of the field. David Coulthard, in third place, trails Senna by over a second and two-tenths. Irvine, in fourth, is nearly two seconds off the pole position time.

As he sips his coffee, he experiences mixed emotions. On one hand, his competitive spirit burns with the desire to go head-to-head with Schumacher and secure a fourth world championship. On the other hand, deep down inside, he knows that this afternoon he will be competing in his 184th and final Grand Prix, regardless of the outcome and even if he loses the title. The weariness of a life spent between airports has overshadowed his love for speed and competition. At 38 years old, a new chapter will begin for him.

At McLaren, they have known since mid-summer that he will retire at the end of the year. He made his final decision after the controversy surrounding Schumacher's penalty at the Silverstone Grand Prix. However, the information has remained secret, and the confirmation of Mika Häkkinen for 1999 has not yet been announced, even though the Finn has been assured of retaining his seat. In order not to disturb him for this decisive Grand Prix, the decision was made to announce Senna's retirement after the race, once the title is secured... or at least that is the hope.

But after the morning warm-up, Ayrton decides to change the previously planned communication strategy with his press officer. He summons the media present at the circuit shortly before noon. In the presence of Ron Dennis and Mika Häkkinen, he confirms the rumor that had been circulating in the paddock for a few weeks. He will retire, definitively this time, after this race, regardless of the outcome, even though he has no doubt that he will leave Suzuka crowned with a fourth world championship title.

By advancing the timing of this announcement, he had the intuition that it would help him find an extra motivation, as everyone now knows that this is his last chance to become champion of the world once again.

Immediately, the press rushes to the Ferrari pit to gather Michael Schumacher's reaction. While acknowledging his opponent's exceptional career, Schumacher states that it changes nothing for this afternoon. He has no intention of giving him a fourth crown as a farewell gift!

During the grid formation, he decides to remain in his seat wearing his famous yellow helmet. Despite the countless displays of sympathy he receives from the other drivers, he hopes to enhance his concentration in this way.

At 2:00 PM, the pack is unleashed for the formation lap. In less than two hours, the world will know the outcome of this 1998 season. But as all the competitors have repositioned themselves at their respective spots, Jarno Trulli waves his arms to signal to the race director that he has stalled. The race director restarts the cars for another formation lap. In the next start, the Prost driver will start from the last position.

After another warm-up lap, the thousands of spectators hold their breath to finally witness the start of the race when they see yellow flags waving at the top of the grid. Unbelievable! Michael Schumacher and Ayrton Senna have stalled almost simultaneously. Their clutches clearly did not appreciate the extended starting procedure. Everything has to be done again, this time with the two championship contenders at the back of the grid!

The real start finally takes place a few minutes later, with an inspired Eddie Irvine immediately taking the lead of the race ahead of Heinz-Harald Frentzen and David Coulthard. There's also no lack of action at the back. At the end of the first lap, Senna is already twelfth with Schumacher hot on his heels. In the next lap, Panis and then Alesi succumb to the attacks of the two furious drivers.

By the end of the fifth lap, Senna is seventh and Schumacher is eighth, but as they climb up the field, their opponents become increasingly difficult to overtake. It takes six laps for the McLaren to pass Damon Hill while keeping an eye on the Ferrari in the rearview mirrors. The Briton, who has no intention of favoring one over the other, resists for two additional laps before diving into the pit lane, giving Schumacher a clear path. The Brazilian takes advantage of his former teammate's resistance to gain a few seconds of advantage over his rival.

On the sixteenth lap, both Senna and Schumacher make pit stops. The McLaren pit stop takes a little longer, and it's ultimately the Ferrari that rejoins the track first, much to Senna's annoyance.

By the twenty-first lap, after the initial pit stops, the standings are as follows: 1. Irvine, 2. Schumacher trailing by 21 seconds, 3. Senna trailing by 22 seconds, 4. Coulthard trailing by 31 seconds. The German has managed to climb back to the provisional podium, which is crucial for him to keep his title chances alive. However, he is still not in control of his own destiny, unless he manages to move up to the first position, and considering the leader is none other than his teammate, it is entirely possible, and Ayrton understands this well. He urgently needs to overtake Schumacher as quickly as possible to protect himself from a Ferrari team strategy.

At this stage of the Grand Prix, the McLaren seems to be performing better than the Ferrari, but Schumacher is fiercely defending his position. Meanwhile, Irvine, who is leading the race, has slowed down, and this doesn't surprise Senna's team.

On the 27th lap, Irvine is called back to the pit lane for a second pit stop, allowing Senna to take the lead ahead of him. In this situation, the title would go to Schumacher by a single point, but there are still over twenty laps to go, and Ayrton is not one to give up easily.

Five laps later, the two contenders, who have been closely marking each other since the start, make simultaneous pit stops once again. Unlike their first stop, they come out of the pits in the same order they entered. The title will have to be decided on the track, much to the delight of the spectators and viewers. At Ferrari, there is a sigh of relief after realizing that one of Schumi's tires was damaged by a carbon debris. Another lap, and his tire would likely have disintegrated.

In his cockpit, Senna is unaware of these developments. He simply observes his prey to choose the best spot to attack. By maintaining pressure on Schumacher, he notices that the German consistently locks up his wheels when braking into the hairpin corner. Therefore, he decides to intensify his pressure at the entry of this tight turn. It's only on the 45th lap that he finally launches a real attack on the Ferrari. Staying close to it in Degner, he swiftly pulls alongside Schumacher during the re-acceleration under the bridge. By the braking point, he is already level with the German, who delays as much as possible before releasing the accelerator for the hairpin. Senna, on the inside, is better positioned to come out in the lead. Schumacher heavily locks up his front wheels and goes into understeer. It's over for him. Senna is in front, and with the flat spots he just created on his tires, Schumacher will have a hard time recovering.

The last five laps are a torment for Michael Schumacher. The vibrations that reach up to his steering column make his car almost undrivable. The rear wing of the McLaren becomes smaller and smaller until it disappears from his field of vision at the start of the final lap.

At the front, Ayrton tries not to think about a possible mechanical failure and prefers to stay focused on his driving. One last passage through Spoon, then through 130R, and here comes the final braking of his last Grand Prix of his career. In the stands, the spectators are in a trance. Seven years after his last title, their hero is going to reclaim the crown at Suzuka.

In the Casio chicane, the stage of his most famous battles with Alain Prost, he takes the time to wave a small gesture to the crowd, then raises his fist as he passes under the checkered flag. It's done. He is a four-time world champion and leaves the sport in the most brilliant way.

On the podium, Schumacher, who has accepted his defeat, applauds the victorious driver with emphasis. He is also celebrating his own immense career, realizing that they will never stand together on a podium again. During the Brazilian national anthem, Ayrton looks down at his mechanics gathered at the foot of the podium. It's then that he locks eyes with a small man with curly hair, wearing a blue shirt, who has also come to applaud him. This time, the story is truly over.

Angra dos Reis, Tuesday, July 13, 1999

Still half asleep as the clock has not yet struck seven in the morning, Ayrton Senna is abruptly awakened by the ringing of his phone. On the other end of the line, he recognizes the voice of a Brazilian journalist friend.

- Good morning, Ayrton. Sorry to disturb you so early, but I needed to know if the information is true, the journalist announces straight to the point, his excitement perceptible in his voice.

Not fully awake yet, Senna doesn't understand the reason for this question and expresses his annoyance.

- What are you talking about, Ricardo?

- It's the Italian newspaper La Stampa that's reporting it in today's edition. They claim that you have agreed to replace Schumacher at Ferrari during his recovery.

Indeed, the German champion had broken his leg in an accident during the first lap of the British Grand Prix the previous Sunday. A double tibia-fibula fracture will keep him away from the tracks for at least three months.

This news immediately shakes Senna out of his
drowsiness.

- I knew that your colleagues sometimes write
  nonsense, but this is beyond belief! Let it be
  known that I haven't been contacted by
  anyone from Ferrari, and I have certainly not
  declared myself a candidate for the seat. I
  hung up my helmet in November, and it's
  final!

- Where could this news possibly come from,
  then? Any ideas?

- Most likely from the overactive imagination of
  some scribbler! he replies.

- I suspected as much, but I'm a bit
  disappointed that it's not true. I would have
  loved to see you in red to conclude your
  career, the journalist expresses his
  disappointment.

- Do you really think I would have accepted to
  play the role of Irvine's lieutenant to help him
  beat Mika? Senna retorts.

- Indeed, looking at the current championship
  standings, you can see that Irvine has scored
  as many points as Schumacher, and Mika is
  still within his reach. I can't imagine Jean Todt
  giving free rein to a replacement and letting

another opportunity to bring the title back to Maranello slip away, Senna explains.

Feeling a bit sheepish, the journalist understands that Senna won't be joining them for the next Grand Prix in Spielberg. Apologizing for disturbing his friend so early, he hangs up.

Annoyed, Senna dives back into his sheets, making sure to turn off his phone to avoid any further interruptions.

Sao Paulo, Monday, January 7, 2013

Sitting in Dr. Almeida's office, a renowned neurologist in Brazil, Ayrton Senna can't hide his impatience and concern. He is waiting for the results of the brain scan he just underwent following a fainting spell during the New Year's Eve party in 2013.

Surrounded by a few close friends, he suddenly collapsed on the table while the party was in full swing. He regained consciousness as the paramedics entered his luxurious villa and was taken to the hospital for a battery of tests.

The creaking of the office door makes him lift his head. The doctor enters the room with a serious expression, carrying a file under his arm. Greeting the former racing driver, he invites him to sit back down in his chair.

- Mr. Senna, I have just come from a meeting with two of my colleagues who have analyzed the images from your brain scan. I won't beat around the bush – we have discovered a mass the size of a lemon in the middle of your brain tissue. It is compressing your brain, which explains your loss of consciousness, says Dr. Almeida.

The doctor couldn't have shocked him more if he had punched him in the face.

- You mean to say that I have a brain tumor, doctor? Ayrton responds, completely stunned by this news.

- Yes, that's correct, I'm afraid. But we need to perform a biopsy to confirm whether it is malignant.

Dumbfounded and slumped in his chair, Ayrton struggles to process the news and remains speechless.

- Have you experienced any headaches or nausea recently? the doctor continues, trying to gather more information.

- Actually, I have been feeling tired, and I've lost my appetite. On New Year's Eve, I couldn't eat much, and I didn't touch my glass of champagne. However, I don't suffer from migraines.

- The symptoms vary depending on the location of the tumor. As for the treatment protocol, I'm afraid we can already exclude surgery. Operating on this part of the brain is very risky and could result in severe motor impairments.

- Do you have any more good news to share, doctor? Senna retorts, slightly annoyed by the clinical coldness of his interlocutor.

- Once we have more information about this tumor, we can consider chemotherapy as a treatment option, which should help shrink it. By the way, I advise you to continue engaging in physical exercise. Recent studies have shown that it enhances the effectiveness of this type of treatment.

Not wanting to prolong his stay in the presence of this professor with undeniably remarkable technical skills but questionable human qualities, Ayrton cuts short this painful visit to return home as soon as possible. Behind the wheel of his car, stuck in traffic, he can't help but melancholically think of his friend, Dr. Sid Watkins, who recently passed away. Trained as a neurologist, he would have surely found the right words to comfort him and guide him towards the best specialists.

Royal London Hospital, Tuesday February 19, 2013

Reluctant to leave his country and loved ones to seek cancer treatment, Ayrton Senna was ultimately persuaded by his friend Ron Dennis to undergo a promising experimental treatment at the Royal London Hospital. Since his initial scan, Dr. Almeida's fears have unfortunately been confirmed. The tumor is malignant and has even grown larger. Increasingly debilitated by the compression on his brain, Ayrton suffers from frequent headaches and episodes of absence. He is now unable to drive alone in his car, as it would pose too great a risk for himself and other road users.

With only his closest confidants aware of his illness and wishing to keep the information from reaching the world at large, he disguises himself with dark glasses and a cap as he approaches the reception desk of the neurology department, headed by Professor Dayton.

Due to privacy concerns, he is immediately directed to a wing of the building reserved for VIPs, and his medical records are filed under an assumed name. On that morning, he begins his chemotherapy treatment and is attended to by a nurse in her forties.

- Hello, Mr. Senna. My name is Kate, and my colleague Leslie and I will be the only ones taking care of you throughout your treatment. We have received strict instructions regarding confidentiality, so you can rest assured that no information will leave this building.

- Thank you, Kate. I trust in your professionalism, Ayrton responds, handing her a small canvas bag marked with the logo of his foundation.

- I heard that you are passionate about racing. Inside this bag, you'll find a few autographed items. I hope you'll enjoy them, he says.

Blushing with emotion, Kate glances into the bag and sees a cap, a fireproof balaclava, and a racing glove used by the champion.

- I don't know what to say. It's so kind of you to think of me, even though we haven't met, she says.

- I believe we'll be seeing each other often in the coming weeks, so we might as well start off on the right foot, Ayrton replies.

- You are in good hands here. The department is internationally renowned, and the treatment prescribed by Professor Dayton is extremely promising.

- I have hope, even though I know my case is

serious. Whatever the outcome, it will be God's will, Ayrton sighs as the nurse places the catheter on his chest, trying to contain her emotions in the presence of the man she has admired since childhood.

- Ayrton... um... may I call you Ayrton? she asks.

- Of course, Kate.

- I know this may not be the best timing, but there's a question that has been weighing on my mind for years, she says.

- Please, go ahead. I have over an hour to wait, and chatting with you will help me take my mind off things, he replies.

- When you abruptly decided to retire in 1994, did the atmosphere within the Williams team contribute to your decision? she asks.

That was almost twenty years ago. On that day in Monaco, I was emotionally at rock bottom. Still not fully recovered from my crash at Imola, the series of serious accidents only worsened my state of mind. Indeed, your intuition was correct. My relationship with Williams wasn't in a good place. After my Imola accident, which was caused by a steering column failure, nobody had the decency to apologize. I could have lost my life, after all! Moreover, during that time at Williams, drivers were considered mere cogs in the machine. Add to that a very challenging car to drive and a lack of motivation, and I didn't need much more to walk away, he explains.

- You could have simply taken a sabbatical year and come back in '95 with another team, she suggests.

- I always said I would have loved to drive for Ferrari, but unfortunately, it never happened. Jean Todt actually contacted me in '95. At that time, I was very occupied with my foundation, and I wasn't thinking much about F1, so I declined the offer. In early '96, my sister lost her husband, and it was very tough for her children. I tried to be there for them as much as possible during those difficult times, which further distanced me from the circuits. When I offered my services to Prost after Panis's accident, the competitive spirit had caught up with me, and I dove back in for an extra season with McLaren, which ultimately became my true family. Looking back, I don't know if I would have built such a relationship with Ferrari. Besides, it couldn't have happened at that time because Schumacher, much younger than me, was the future for the Scuderia.

- Speaking of Schumacher, I was wondering what your opinion of him is?

- When he first arrived, I won't hide that I despised him. His arrogance and dirty tricks annoyed me. But during our duel in 1998, he proved to be a formidable yet fair opponent. He's not among my closest friends, but we have great respect for each other and enjoy seeing each other on the circuits. His track record speaks for itself. He's an exceptional driver who would have further solidified his place in history by battling against a driver of his caliber starting from 2000.

- And among the current drivers, who do you appreciate the most?

- Of course, there's Bruno, my nephew, for whom I have a lot of affection, and I've supported him to reach the highest level. But apart from family ties, I would say that Lewis Hamilton resembles me a lot. He's a pure attacker who would accumulate world titles if he has a competitive car. For obvious reasons, I have a great fondness for Felipe Massa. His accident in 2009 dealt a severe setback to his progress, and since then, he's not quite the same driver.

- And Vettel, who has been winning world titles for three years?

- His maturity at such a young age has always amazed me. He's brilliant, and for the sake of the spectacle, I dream of a duel between him and Hamilton. It would remind me of our great moments with Alain!

- I would love to continue this conversation

with you, Ayrton, but I have to leave now. Other patients are waiting for me. We'll see each other again next week, anyway.

- Until next time, Kate. It was a pleasure to chat with a true Formula 1 fan!

Monaco, F1 Grand Prix, May 25-26, 2013

The news shakes the entire Monaco Grand Prix paddock. In today's edition, an English tabloid reveals to the world that Ayrton Senna is suffering from a serious brain illness and is currently being treated in a London hospital. In the tight-knit world of F1, only a few rare insiders were aware of the Brazilian champion's health condition and had managed to keep the information secret until now.

Three months after the start of his chemotherapy, Ayrton's health has improved. Examinations have shown a significant reduction in the size of the tumor, and although exhausted from this aggressive treatment, he has regained greater mobility. However, the doctors have warned him that the path to recovery will be long and challenging.

Now that the world is aware of his illness, Ayrton no longer has a reason to hide, and to prevent any attempts at paparazzi photographs, he decides to fly to the Principality for a surprise visit to the stands of his favorite Grand Prix.

As soon as he enters the paddock, news of his arrival spreads like wildfire. Within minutes, dozens of photographers and cameramen gather around him. Despite the chaos, Ayrton strolls from one team's pit to another, happily reconnecting with some old acquaintances.

The illness has transformed the silhouette of the former world champion. He has lost a significant amount of weight, and his balding head is concealed under a cap. Niki Lauda, always playful, remarks that they are now equal in that aspect. But despite the façade of good humor, the atmosphere remains heavy in the paddock of the Monaco circuit. The sight of this immense champion so diminished is particularly shocking for those who knew him at the height of his glory.

Méribel, French Alps, Sunday, December 29, 2013

As he has done for several years, Michael Schumacher spends the end-of-year holidays in his chalet in Méribel, in the French Alps. With his wife Corinna and their two children, Gina Maria, 16 years old, and Mick, 14 years old, he enjoys the ski resort of the elegant Savoyard station. More than a year after his second retirement from racing, the eight-time world champion, who will celebrate his 45th birthday in a few days, is an active retiree who divides his time between his various residences. Being very sporty, he maintains his physical condition as he always did during his racing career.

Like Ayrton, he made a comeback to competition after a first retirement following the 2006 Brazilian Grand Prix. But unlike Ayrton, his return ended in a bitter failure. Dominated in all aspects by his teammate Nico Rosberg during their three seasons together at Mercedes, he definitively left the sport at the end of 2012 through the back door. These additional 58 Grands Prix only allowed him to add a single podium at Valencia in 2012 and a fastest lap to his immense list of achievements.

Now freed from all media and sporting pressure, as well as any professional commitments, he simply enjoys life with his family and friends.

This Sunday morning, the weather is promising in Savoie. Michael plans to ski as soon as the slopes open, accompanied by his son and a group of friends. The first rays of sunshine pierce through the windows of his chalet as the German champion sits down at the table to have a hearty breakfast. The day will be intense, and he needs to store up some calories.

In front of his steaming cup of coffee, he absentmindedly checks the news of the day on his tablet. Amused by the story of a New York gardener who found a winning lottery ticket in a pile of leaves, his attention is then drawn to the announcement of a fifth death in four days in the French Alps. All the victims were killed in avalanches while skiing off-piste. As a protective father, he can't help but remind Mick of the safety instructions, even though they don't plan to venture off the marked slopes and the risk seems minimal.

It's just 9 o'clock when he leaves the table, satisfied, to get dressed and prepare his equipment. Being a fan of new technologies, he equips his helmet with a mini camera that will capture some beautiful memories of this day.

After bidding Corinna a final goodbye with a kiss, the father and son are ready to join their friends at the base of the chairlift. But as soon as they step out the door, Michael's mobile phone rings. Taking off his gloves, he sees that it's his friend Jean Todt calling.

The Frenchman, freshly reelected as the head of the International Automobile Federation, had long been in charge of the Scuderia Ferrari, with which Michael achieved his greatest successes. Together, they secured six drivers' world championships (1997, 2000, 2001, 2002, 2003, and 2004) and celebrated 72 victories in red. Since then, a deep friendship has formed between the two men, who frequently call each other, although this early morning phone call intrigues the former Ferrari driver.

- Hello, Jean.

- Good morning, Michael.

- What's happening that you're calling me so early on a Sunday morning?

- Unfortunately, it's not good news.

- You're worrying me, Jean...

- Ron Dennis just called me... Ayrton passed away barely an hour ago. That damn cancer won the battle.

Although he knew his former rival was seriously ill, the latest news he had received was rather encouraging. This sudden announcement takes his breath away. Overwhelmed by emotions, he cuts the conversation short with his friend and goes back inside the chalet. With teary eyes, he informs Corinna of the news and collapses onto the couch. Even though they weren't very close, this loss affects him much more than he could have imagined. With Ayrton, a part of his past glory also departs.

Resting on the coffee table, his phone keeps vibrating. Journalists, who have also learned about the Brazilian's death, are trying to reach him to gather his initial statements.

To put an end to this harassment, he decides to answer and give them what they want. Interview after interview, the minutes pass by.

Feeling too overwhelmed to handle it, he then asks Corinna to inform their friends. Given the circumstances, the planned day of skiing is, of course, canceled.

Imola the day after

ANNEXES

World championship standings

1997

		1	2	3	4	5	6	7	8	9	10	11	12	13	14	15	16	17	Pts
		AUS	BRA	ARG	SMR	MCO	ESP	CAN	FRA	GBR	DEU	HUN	BEL	ITA	AUT	LUX	JPN	EUR	
1	M. SCHUMACHER	6	2	-	6	10	3	10	10	-	4	3	10	1	1	-	10	4	80
2	J. VILLENEUVE	-	10	10	-	-	10	-	2	10	-	10	2	2	10	10	-	3	79
3	H. FRENTZEN	-	-	-	10	-	-	3	4	-	-	-	4	4	4	4	6	-	39
4	D. COULTHARD	10	-	-	-	-	1	-	-	3	-	-	-	10	6	-	-	6	36
5	J. ALESI	-	1	-	2	-	4	6	1	6	1	-	-	6	-	6	2	-	35
6	G. BERGER	3	6	1	-	-	-			10	-	1	-	-	3	-	2		26
7	M. HAKKINEN	4	3	2	1	-	-	-	-	-	3	-	-	-	-	-	3	10	26
8	E. IRVINE	-	-	6	4	4	-	-	3	-	-	-	-	-	-	-	4	1	22
9	G. FISICHELLA	-	-	-	3	1	-	4	-	-	-	-	6	3	3	-	-	-	20
10	O. PANIS	2	4	-	-	3	6	-								1	-	-	16
11	J. HERBERT	-	-	3	-	-	2	2	-	-	-	4	3	-	-	-	1	-	15
12	A. SENNA							6	-	6	2	-	-	-					14
13	R. SCHUMACHER	-	-	4	-	-	-	-	-	2	2	1	-	-	2	-	-	-	11
14	D. HILL	-	-	-	-	-	-	-	-	1	-	6	-	-	-	-	-	-	7
15	R. BARRICHELLO	-	-	-	-	6	-	-	-	-	-	-	-	-	-	-	-	-	6
16	A. WURZ							-	-	4									4
17	P. DINIZ	-	-	-	-	-	-	-	-	-	-	-	-	-	-	2	-	-	2
18	M. SALO	-	-	-	-	2	-	-	-	-	-	-	-	-	-	-	-	-	2
19	S. NAKANO	-	-	-	-	-	-	1	-	-	-	-	-	-	-	-	-	-	1
20	N. LARINI	1	-	-	-	-													1

1998

		1	2	3	4	5	6	7	8	9	10	11	12	13	14	15	16	Pts
		AUS	BRA	ARG	SMR	ESP	MCO	CAN	FRA	GBR	AUT	DEU	HUN	BEL	ITA	LUX	JPN	
1	A. SENNA	10	10	6	-	10	10	-	-	6	10	10	1	-	6	10	10	99
2	M. SCHUMACHER	-	4	10	6	4	-	10	10	10	4	2	10	-	10	6	6	92
3	D. COULTHARD	6	6	1	10	6	-	-	2	-	6	6	6	-	-	4	3	56
4	E. IRVINE	3	-	4	4	-	4	4	6	4	3	-	-	-	4	3	4	43
5	J. VILLENEUVE	2	-	-	3	1	2	-	4	-	1	4	4	-	-	-	-	21
6	D. HILL	-	-	-	-	-	-	-	-	-	-	3	3	10	1	-	2	19
7	A. WURZ	-	3	3	-	3	-	3	3	3	-	-	-	-	-	-	-	18
8	G. FISICHELLA	4	2	-	2	-	-	-	-	-	-	-	2	3	-	2	1	16
9	H. FRENTZEN	-	1	-	-	-	6	6	-	2	-	-	-	-	-	1	-	16
10	R. SCHUMACHER	-	-	-	-	-	-	-	-	1	2	1	-	6	3	-	-	13
11	J. ALESI	-	-	2	1	-	-	-	1	-	-	-	-	4	2	-	-	10
12	R. BARRICHELLO	-	-	-	-	2	-	2	-	-	-	-	-	-	-	-	-	4
13	M. SALO	-	-	-	-	-	3	-	-	-	-	-	-	-	-	-	-	3
14	P. DINIZ	-	-	-	-	-	1	-	-	-	-	-	-	2	-	-	-	3
15	J. HERBERT	1	-	-	-	-	-	-	-	-	-	-	-	-	-	-	-	1
16	J. TRULLI	-	-	-	-	-	-	-	-	-	-	-	-	1	-	-	-	1
17	J. MAGNUSSEN	-	-	-	-	-	-	1										1

Imola the day after

Dear readers,

You have purchased this book on Amazon, and I encourage you to share your reader review on the sales website.

If you wish to contact me: ilariopax@gmail.com

Thank you for your support and feedback.

Best regards,

Imola the day after

Printed in Great Britain
by Amazon